Keep the closet closed... and other ghost stories

Keep the closet closed

and other ghost stories

by

Esther J. Hervy

translated by Jacquie Bridonneau

Short stories

2018

At the Truck Stop

It looked like this July day was going to be a nice one. The Ambroise family had set off early this morning and everyone was looking forward to arriving in Joyeuse, a little village nestled in the middle of the countryside of the Ardèche, in the south of France. Olivier, the father, was driving down the tollway while Julia, the mother, often looked at the back seat to glance at Salome, their daughter, who had fallen asleep, hugging Lola, her doll, against her chest. It was nearly half past twelve and they had been driving for almost two hours now. This tollway had just been inaugurated, and most of the full-service rest areas and truck stops had only partially been opened. They had passed a few places where they might have stopped for lunch, but they didn't seem to have been equipped with all the modern equipment you usually find in truck stops on freeways nowadays. No, Olivier had repeated this to Julia, he wanted to have lunch in a real restaurant and had decided to go the twenty more miles to get to one. Julia looked at her husband and said:

"She looks just like an angel, don't you think?"
Olivier glanced in the rear-view mirror and smiled. His daughter, his baby girl Salome: seven years old, wavy brown hair falling on both sides of her face with its pale white skin, a little smile on her lips when she was dreaming. And those huge blue eyes you'd see when she woke up. Had someone been casting a little girl to play Snow White, Salome would have been first pick, that's for sure!
 "She looks like you more and more," said Olivier to his wife. "But a little younger and fresher," he continued.
"You bastard!" Julia said, pretending to hit him. "Always the ladies' man, aren't you?"
Olivier took Julia's hand and brought it to his lips to kiss it.
"But you'll always be my beloved little wife."
« Oh. Well isn't that nice of you honey. A real gentleman. »
They kept on talking and joking, while the little car was driving down the nearly deserted tollway, taking them closer to their cottage in the countryside. Those twenty miles went by quickly and the little black car's blinker told the few vehicles following them that they were turning onto the deceleration lane to get ready to turn off. Contrary though to the tollway, the truck stop was teeming with people. All the parking spaces were already taken by cars, vans and camping cars. Lots of drivers had even parked on the sidewalks in order to squeeze into a place. Olivier drove up and

down and finally was lucky enough to score a parking spot when someone pulled out just in front of him.

"It looks like it's our lucky day!" he said to Julia.

He put on the parking brake and turned the car off. In the back seat, Salome opened her eyes. Two deep blue marbles, as blue as the waters in a mountain lake, opened up, astonished. Still half asleep, the little girl looked out the back window.

"I'm hungry Daddy," she said, with a yawn.

"Daddy's starving too sweetie."

Julia and Olivier got out of the car and while Olivier was locking it up, Julia undid Salome's seatbelt. She picked her up, closed the back door and put Salome back down onto the hot asphalt. The three of them started off towards the restaurant, the little girl running ahead. When they opened the doors, they could immediately smell all sorts of tasty fragrances coming from the kitchens: exotic mixtures of various types, herbs, spices and other condiments blended one with the other subtlety.

"What, this is a truck stop restaurant?" Julia asked, astonished.

Olivier nodded, wondering the same thing. It's true that this place seemed to be anything except a restaurant you'd find on a freeway. Round tables were covered with elegant white lace-trimmed tablecloths and had big black chandeliers in the center. Fine porcelain dishes sparkled, reflecting the silverware. The walls were covered in red wall hangings, making the restaurant feel opulent and cozy. In spite of the heat outside in this month of July in the south of France, inside it was cool and pleasant. There wasn't a self-service area like you find in most truck stop restaurants, but rather servers wearing black suits and white shirts, taking orders and coming and going from the kitchens.

"Wow," exclaimed Salome. "It's like we're in a castle here!"

"A castle for my little princess!" answered her father, picking her up.

While they were admiring the restaurant, a man wearing a white shirt and black pleated trousers came up to them.

"Ladies, Sir, if you could please follow me."

Olivier and Julia both looked at each other, like they didn't believe what was happening. They obediently followed the server who led them to a small table. Grinning, Julia glanced at him. What kind of place was this anyway? She had never seen anything like it in her entire life. Such high-class fixtures for a truck stop on a freeway, this was just ridiculous actually. But anyway, what was important was that they were going to get something to eat and would be able to continue their trip down south, nice and full and relaxed. After all, it was much more pleasant to have lunch in a place like this rather than stopping in one of those sad snack bars with pallid lighting that you usually find off the freeways... even though, they both had to admit, this place was slightly peculiar.

Though the restaurant seemed upper class, the menu was a quite traditional one. They both ordered a grilled steak and salad and Salome had the under-12 menu with fried chicken and French fries, served with a large glass of pomegranate juice and mineral water for the couple.

"Why should we regret not having a glass of Bordeaux when we've got such pure water in our glasses?" joked Olivier, clinking his glass against Julia's in a mock toast.

"Look Daddy, I've got wine!" said Salome with a smile, lifting her glass with the reddish pomegranate syrup in it.

"Well I guess that means that we're not going to let you drive to take us on vacation then."

"But Daddy, I don't know how to drive yet," she answered, seriously.

The server came with their meals and they all readily dug in. The restaurant was full of a pleasant hustle and bustle and everyone seemed to be enjoying themselves. You could hear glasses clinking together in toasts and cutlery clicking against the immaculate plates. Adults were talking about this, that and the other, while children, napkins around their necks, had their noses to the plates, eating just like cute little ogres. Julia suddenly realized at all these people seemed to be wearing their Sunday best, which was weird for people driving to their vacation get-aways. She was just going to mention this to her husband when Salome butted in:

"Mom, look at that little kitty over there!" She pointed her finger towards the forest that could be seen through the window. Julia and Olivier turned their heads in the direction their daughter was indicating. A tabby cat was sitting under a tree and looking right at them.

"Mom, can I go and pet it? Can I?"

And she was right, this cat was looking at them, you could even say it was staring at them! The feline finally did get up though and went off into the woods.

"Oh no Mom, it's gone! I want to go out and see it!"

"You finish eating first sweetie, we'll go out and pet it if it comes back before we leave," said Olivier. Salome, disappointed and almost pouting, picked up a fry with her fork. Olivier ruffled her hair with a smile, but the little girl pulled away.

"Don't worry, we'll go see the little kitty when we're finished eating." Salome looked at her father with her big blue eyes.

"Promise ?"

"Yes, promise. But first, finish eating."

The little girl finished up her plate, visibly reassured. The meal had been a simple one, though totally delicious. The whole family had really enjoyed it and while Salome was finishing up her scoop of chocolate ice-cream, Julia went to the restroom. She opened the door and went in. No one was there. The restroom was clean and nicely decorated, just like the rest of the restaurant:

elegant and a bit vintage. The walls were covered in pale pink tiles. There was a huge mirror with a delicate black wrought iron border above the two spic and span white porcelain sinks. Julia went into one of the stalls and when she was about to leave, she heard someone opening the door and going into the neighboring stall. She left and went towards the sinks to wash her hands. She looked at herself in the mirror. Her pale white skin contrasted with her dark brown hair. Her daughter did look a lot like her. The same big blue eyes, the same thin delicate nose. Despite the fatigue she had accumulated at work throughout the entire year, which could be seen on her tired and drawn features, Julia remained an exceptionally beautiful young woman. She smiled at her reflection, as if she was persuading herself of this, turned off the water and dried her hands. When she was almost ready to go back to the restaurant, she heard a sob coming from the other side of the occupied stall. She stopped and listened. There was someone who was crying in there. She felt like an idiot, standing in the middle of the ladies' room, listening to someone she didn't know who was crying. Should she knock on the door, to make sure she was all right? Or on the other hand, should she just leave, as if nothing was happening, because after all she didn't know this lady and it was none of her business anyway? She didn't have much time to make up her mind though, as the stall door opened. Julia rushed back to the sink and turned the water on. She felt like she had been caught red-handed in the act of voyeurism. She didn't even know why she hadn't just left. Undoubtedly because of the curiosity to know what this mysterious lady who was alleviating her sorrows in the lady's room in a truck stop looked like. The bathroom stall door opened and a nice-looking blond lady came out. She came towards Julia without even looking at her and turned on the water in the second sink. She looked just like she had stepped out of the 50s. Her platinum-blond and wavy hair reached her shoulders and framed her face, highlighting her scarlet-red lipstick and black false eyelashes. She looked just like a Hollywood starlet. Her transparent skin was porcelain white. She took off her black gloves and put her perfectly manicured hands under the water. The young lady kept her head down, undoubtedly out of modesty. She probably didn't want someone she didn't know to see how upset she was, here in a place that was so commonplace and unexpected as a truck stop off the freeway. She sighed deeply and turned off the water. She picked up her purse, or to be exact, her golden handbag, and took a tube of lipstick out. She raised her head, making eye contact with Julia in the mirror. Her eyes were cold and sad and were emerald-colored. Julia looked down, turned off the water and quickly wiped her hands. She turned around and left while the pin-up was refreshing her scarlet red lipstick. When she got back to the table, Julia told Olivier about what happened in the bathroom with this strange looking lady.

"And you should have seen the suit she was wearing!" she said, "it was incredibly elegant. I mean I had the impression that I was acting in one of those black and white movies in the beginning of the 50s!"

She looked for that blond lady, hoping she'd be able to point her out to her husband. Unfortunately, she was nowhere to be seen in the restaurant. Perhaps the starlet had locked herself in to evacuate her heartache, far from the noise and happy people eating in the restaurant?

"Mom?"

Salome woke Julia up from her daydreaming.

"What do you want honey?"

"Can I play on the slide outside?"

Julia looked at Olivier, who looked outside through the window. They could both see the slide from their table and could consequently watch their daughter, while having a cup of coffee. After that, they'd go back on the tollway quickly.

"Go ahead honey. But make sure you stay on this side, so that Mummy and Daddy can see you, okay?"

"Okay Mom!"

And the little girl jumped off her seat and ran to the door. Julia watched her leave.

"I'm going to go to the bathroom," said Olivier, getting up. "I'll pay and order two cups of coffee while I'm up."

Julia nodded her head. While Olivier was walking

towards the bathroom, she watched Salome play, going up and down the slide, having fun like only little kids know how to do. Having fun, without ever stopping, without ever getting tired. Then, while Julia was admiring her daughter having fun outside, she saw the blond lady on the other side of the parking lot, walking briskly. Julia turned around to see if Olivier was back but couldn't find him. Though of course she couldn't hear anything, just by looking at the way her hips were swaying, Julia could imagine the dry clicking sounds that her heels must have been making on the hot asphalt in the parking lot. And it was so weird, she must have been boiling in this black and tightly fitted suit. Wearing nylon stockings too. Like didn't she feel laced up in this party costume? This outfit seemed totally out of line with the venue (after all, this was just a truck stop off a tollway!), that Julia ended up wondering if the young lady wasn't driving off to some sort of thematic costume night or something. Salome noticed the lady in her seamed stockings and stopped playing. She stared at her, as if she had seen a full-scale doll. Her eyes followed her as she kept on walking. Her hips swayed from right to left, she almost looked like a feline. Strangely enough though, no one seemed to notice her. It was as if only Julia and her daughter had seen this beauty straight out from the olden days. She seemed to know where she was headed, and alone, she winded her way through the other people, as if she blended into them naturally. All of a sudden she stopped. Her face seemed to light up when she saw the cat that they had seen at the beginning of their meal. Julia saw her say something but couldn't hear her. She had probably called the animal. She quickly walked towards it, but the cat bolted off into the woods. The lady quickened her step and then she also disappeared into the woods. Julia didn't know what to think of all this. Who was this lady? And what was she doing here, all dressed up like this and following a yellow tabby cat into the woods? Olivier was getting ready to leave the restroom to join his wife and have a cup of coffee before setting off again, when he heard someone talking to him:

"Excuse me."

He turned his head and saw a beautiful blond lady, her eyes begging him.

"Sir, please. My cat ran away. Did you happen to see it?"

This ludicrous almost made Olivier burst out into laugher, but the lady seemed so sad and serious that he changed his mind. She continued:

"I lost it yesterday, after the show. You understand, it's all I've got left. It's all I've got left of her."

Then Olivier remembered the cat that Salome had seen when they were having lunch.

"Yes, I did see a cat a while ago. It went into the woods."

The lady's eyes lit up.

"Here, I'll show you where I saw it if you want. It was a yellow tabby cat, wasn't it?" he continued, while walking down the hall that led to the restaurant. "That was it, wasn't it Ma'am?" he repeated.

As she didn't answer, Olivier turned around. The lady had disappeared, and no one was following him. He was taken aback for a few seconds. Looked to the right, then to the left. Went back to the bathrooms but the good-looking blond lady had disappeared. Olivier looked around once again, as if she might appear suddenly at any time, then realizing that no one was there, went back to his table. When he arrived, he sat down and leaned towards Julia and said:

"You'll never believe this!"

"I won't believe what?" answered Julia, raising an eyebrow.

"Your blond lady. I think I saw her."

"In the bathroom?"

"And she even spoke to me."

"That's impossible, I saw her outside not even thirty seconds ago. And that cat we were talking about, I think it's hers, she was running after it."

Olivier's throat tightened up.

"She asked me if I had seen her cat."

Julia looked at him, astonished.

"What did she look like?"

"Like that..." said Olivier weakly, pointing at the window.

The blond lady was outside with Salome. She was

talking to her and caressing her face. Salome seemed neither worried nor frightened. She just looked at her with her big blue eyes, like she was admiring her. However, the young blond lady didn't seem to be talking directly to Salome. Of course, she was talking to her, but her eyes, even though they were aimed at her, were unarguably empty. Olivier and Julia ran out of the restaurant as fast as they could. When they reached the slide, the little girl was alone once again.

"Sweetie, who was that lady talking to you?" asked Julia anxiously.

"That was Betty, she was looking for her cat."

"Betty ?" repeated Olivier.

"Yup, and she also told me that I looked like her little girl, Abigail," added Salome with a smile.

"All right, we've got to go now," said Julia.

"But the cat, Mom? You said that we could see it before leaving," protested Salome.

"But the cat's gone now honey. We have to leave now if we want to get there in time to check into the apartment. Remember? We're going on vacation. You don't feel like swimming in the pool and going on walks in the mountains?"

"Of course Mom, but the kitty... I want to pet it. Betty told me she'd give it to me if I was good!"

"Okay, we're heading off to the car right now!" said Olivier, raising his voice. "Let's go, let's go, we've already wasted enough time as it is."

And he started off towards the car, inviting them to follow. Julia pretended to follow him, turning around to see Salome's reaction. She followed them, resigned, though she was pouting, showing them her disagreement. She turned around to look at the slide, looking for the cat, visibly disappointed by her parents' reactions. "What the heck just happened here? And who the hell was this lady?" added Olivier when Julia caught up with him.

"I have no idea... I've got a funny feeling about her and I don't like it."

"Everyone get into the car. Salome, hurry up!"

A deafening and unexpected thunderclap rang out and Julia gasped, startled.

"Hurry up honey," she said, turning around to talk to her daughter, who was no longer behind her.

The sun hid itself behind dark clouds, as if ripped out of the sky by the electrical burst. The temperature fell by several degrees and a brisk wind appeared, making the tall trees off the parking lot sway. Julia's heart stopped beating for a few seconds while she was trying to get Salome's attention. Her breathing became short and irregular. She broke out into a sweat, in spite of the wind and the drop in temperature.

"Salome, where are you?" she shouted, her heart beating loudly and irregularly. "Over there!" answered Olivier, pointing at the restaurant door.

Julia looked in the direction her husband had indicated, and before the restaurant doors closed on her daughter's brown wavy hair, she only had enough time to make out an elegant gloved hand on her head.

"Hey ! You! Don't you touch my daughter!"

Olivier ran to the restaurant, shouting. When he got to the doors and wanted to open them, it was impossible: they were locked. Julia ran up to him.

"Where is she?" she screamed to her husband.

Olivier didn't pay any attention to his wife and ran towards the window. He scrunched up his hands in front of his eyes, looking inside. The restaurant wasn't anything at all like it had been just a few minutes earlier. For one thing, it was empty. All the vacationers had disappeared, like they had been swept away, or vanished, or even kidnapped (but by who, or by what)? The restaurant was dark, commonplace and cold. Even from the outside, you could smell a thick layer of dust in the air. The plates that remained on the tables were dirty, with uneaten food stuck to the formerly spotlessly clean porcelain in greenish and brownish stains. Colonies of ants ran up and down on the table and chair legs, in a disordered ballet, voraciously scurrying to these moldy leftovers before the others got there.

"What the hell is going on here?"

"Where is she?" shouted Julia once again when she reached the window.

Olivier didn't answer. He bent down and picked up a large stone from the ground.

"Move over!" he ordered his wife so she'd back away. Her eyes full of apprehension, Julia stepped back. Olivier threw the stone at the window pane.

The explosion of breaking glass resonated in the deafening silence surrounding them. The echo bounced off the walls of the building, then off the trees and finally was lost in the dark clouds full of electricity that obstructed the sky. Olivier ran up to the opening he had just made and climbed through the broken window. Julia followed him closely, but despite her maternal instinct ordering her to do everything possible to find her daughter, she hesitated for a brief second. Another instinct, this one even more primary, was trying to warn her and order her to turn back. A little voice that she could barely make out was ordering her to be careful and begging her not to let herself be swallowed by this mouth that only had one thing in mind: devouring them. She told it to shut up and followed her husband into the restaurant. Now both of them were standing inside the broken window and their heels were both covered in shards of glass. They had reached the other side, they were now unable to undo what they had just done.

"But where are we?" whispered Julia softly to herself.

"Salome!" shouted out Olivier, walking through the tables and looking left and right, completely stunned by this new world surrounding them.

"Salome!" repeated Julia, who remained unable to move, next to the broken glass from the window where they both crawled in. A nightmare, but she was awake! What was this new universe where they had both landed? Olivier ran to the back of the restaurant without paying any attention to his wife, who finally mustered her courage and joined him, on her tiptoes. There was electricity in the air and this unsettling and peculiar impression of not being alone in this abandoned restaurant. Of course, this wasn't because her husband was with her. A strange impression of calmness bounced off the walls and beat against her ears. She made sure she didn't near the large drapes hanging from the windows. Her senses were alerted, her brain was telling her that this was an emergency. The dark and heavy curtains were projecting strange and worrying shadows on the floor. But had shadows ever hurt anyone? I don't think so. Now though, Julia was no longer sure that they were both in a real situation. She preferred to avoid them while trying to catch up with Olivier. They stopped running when they reached the restrooms. There was a poster on the door. A poster for a cabaret. Olivier ripped it off and looked at it.

"What the heck?" "Jesus Christ!" added Julia, looking over his shoulder. Olivier was holding a piece of paper that seemed to date back several decades. Pictured on it was the blond lady they had both seen, wearing a corset and black nylons, holding a boa in one hand and a cigarette holder in the other. The colors of the photo were so faded that the pin-up's skin seemed to be dull and dirty. Consequently, with this photo of a young debutante, you could imagine an old lady who was ready to hatch. A reddish tabby cat was standing at her feet, smiling and raising its head to admire her.

"Betty. It's Betty on this poster! And she kidnapped our daughter!" shouted Olivier, throwing the poster down. Julia bent over to pick it up while her husband went to check out the kitchens. She folded it and put it in her back pocket.

"Olivier! Olivier, wait for me!" Olivier pushed the kitchen door open. He went in and ran around the large stoves, bending down and looking everyplace where his daughter could have possibly been.

"Olivier!" His wife stood still at the kitchen doors, looking at him hopelessly.

"I swear I'll find her if it's the last thing I do!" he said, without even looking at her while continuing to search through the kitchens.

"Olivier, stop it! Stop it now!" she screamed. He stood up and looked at her, with stupefaction.

"Can't you see that something's wrong here? Can't you see that nothing is the same now?" Olivier looked at her, surprised, and they looked around the room.

"What I mean," continued Julia, "what I mean is that I've got the impression that we're not in the same place. Or rather, no longer in the same place... not the same geographical place, but the same place... in time?" She had pronounced this last word carefully and with hesitation. She took the poster out of her pocket and held it out so her husband could see it. Olivier looked at it and then raised his eyes to look at Julia.

"Who is this lady?" whispered Olivier, almost to himself.

"I have no idea. But when I ran into her in the bathroom before, it was like she had come out of a different era. I don't understand. I don't know where (when?) we are, I don't understand why this lady is following us and I don't know why she's interested in our little girl. Olivier, I want to find our daughter, I'm scared, I'm so scared..."

Olivier put his arms around his wife and hugged her. He could feel his wife's warm tears on his cold skin, running down his neck. In spite of the warmth of Julia's body against his, he shivered. He looked towards the back of the kitchen, towards the dark hall leading to the bathrooms. There was nobody there. However, he could feel a presence right at this very spot. A presence observing them and enjoying their disarray. Olivier trembled and hugged his wife even tighter against his chest. She finally stopped sobbing and pulled away. He pushed her hair out of her face and dried a tear on one of her cheeks with the back of his hand.

"We'll find her, I promise." When they left the kitchens, the hall was lit up. Light was coming from the restaurant. Olivier took Julia's arm and pushed her behind him. Sticking close to the wall, he advanced carefully.

"You stay behind me," he whispered to his wife. Julia stuck close to him, putting her feet right in his footsteps. The temperature hadn't increased, but pungent drops of sweat were running down his backbone. Julia felt feverish and febrile. Her muscles were so tight that her whole body was aching. Her stiff legs moved automatically, in tune with Olivier's steps.

"I think I heard something," he said. Julia stopped, wary and alert.

"I think it's coming from the bathroom," he continued. Julia looked towards the door at the end of the hall. She held her breath, trying to make as little noise as possible. Olivier looked at her, his finger sur his lips. He was holding his breath too. They slowly tiptoed to the door and when Olivier put his arm to reach the door handle, it opened wide all by itself, as if some sort of invisible and driven force had pushed it open from the inside. Olivier jumped back automatically, and Julia uttered a cry of surprise, hanging on even harder to her husband's arm, who because of his unexpected movement, almost knocked her over. The thick layer of makeup on her face wasn't enough to conceal the sadness emanating from her eyes. Her long black lashes closed slowly, masking and showing her deep blue and pure irises. Her blond and wavy hair barely moved. At this instant, she embodied femininity. Femininity and eroticism, but in an elegant and sensual way. When she reached Julia and Olivier, she sighed, as if she were resigned. Olivier tried to catch her arm, but his hand went right through it, as if Betty were a mere illusion. Julia was unable to move, her eyes and mouth wide open. Both of them, still leaning against the wall that had prevented them from falling, stared at her, watching her disappear behind the door frame that led to the restaurant. They could hear some jazz, followed by heavy applause. A man's voice belted out from the microphone:

"And now, Ladies and Gentlemen, just for you tonight, the most divine, the most sensual, and the most beautiful of our pinups, Mademoiselle Betty!" Julia was the one who moved first. Olivier immediately followed her. They looked through the door, not believing what they were seeing: the restaurant was full. The people, all wearing their Sunday best, were staring at Betty on stage. And at the feet of the chair, right at the center of the stage, the yellow tabby cat was sitting. The very same cat that Salome wanted to pet. Olivier was sure of it.

"Look !" Olivier said to Julia, pointing at the cat. "That's the cat I saw before!" Olivier stepped forward, but Julia pulled him back.

"Wait a second!" she said. "This isn't possible."

"What, what are you talking about?" he said, pulling away from her.

"Look... I mean, just look at them..."

"What do you mean..."

Olivier looked at the people in the audience. Everyone was smiling. Even more than smiling actually... they were guffawing. They were laughing so much that their jaws were undone. They were laughing, coughing and spitting onto their plates and their Sunday best clothing. They were suffocating. But what was the most worrying, was what they were looking at. These people weren't looking at the stage or at Mademoiselle Betty and her little strip show; they were staring at both of them, intensely and not the least bit embarrassed about it. Olivier stepped back.

"Back up, Julia, back up!" But Julia surprisingly started shouting:

"Where is my daughter? Give me my daughter back!" She was so panicked that her eyeballs seemed to be popping out of their orbits, and her features, usually so regular and delicate, suddenly seemed harsh and vulgar. She continued:

"My daughter, tell me what you did with my daughter!" And she ran to the stage. That's when the audience stopped laughing. The projectors were turned off and the music stopped. Julia stood still. She looked at Betty. The dancer had stopped her strip show as soon as the music stopped playing. The supple and gracious cat curled itself around Betty's black heels. It sat down, and stared at Julia, with its big almost human-looking green eyes. It started purring so loud that even Olivier could hear it from where he was standing.

"Tony's not going to like this, you know," said Betty, on a monotonous tone.

"What are you talking about?" sputtered Julia. The audience didn't move. You could even say that they were all holding their breath, attentively watching what was happening between these two protagonists who were acting out a key scene in a play in front of them, not wanting to miss a single thing.

"Tony," repeated Betty, her head pointing to the back of the room. Julia and Olivier turned their heads at the same time in the direction Betty had indicated. In the very back of the theater, a man of imposing stature was leaning against a large window. Smoke from his cigar was rising, forming circles around him, as if his evil aura was escaping from the pores of his skin. He sneered maliciously and then walked towards the stage to address Betty: "So? Where is she?" Effortlessly and almost like a feline, Betty weaved her way around the tables. "She's here Tony, she's here. Don't worry, I did it." The cat meowed, loudly.

"Give us our daughter back!" shouted Olivier, running towards his wife. Tony looked at the couple, almost casually, as if this was not important, and answered:

"Don't worry, you'll get her back."

"Right now!" Julia shouted to him, tears running down her cheeks.

"But before that," continued Tony, "we've got something to do."

"You bastard..." screamed Olivier, stepping towards him.

"Don't move!" ordered Tony, opening a side of his jacket, revealing the buttstock of a revolver that he was ready to use. Olivier stopped in his tracks. The spectators remained open-mouthed, almost drooling in front of this breathtaking representation. "Yes, we've got something to do, don't we Betty?" Betty nodded. She went back to the cat that had been sitting on the front of the stage, without budging, and picked it up.

"Come here, my little one, it's over. You're going back to Mummy and Daddy. Everything's going to be like it used to be."

Tony joined the dancer on the stage, still pointing his gun towards Julia and Olivier, both horrified by what was happening. Then, turning around to address the audience, Tony shouted out a thundering:

"Let the show begin!"

He stepped aside. Betty went to the front of the scene and started singing a song with strange words. At her feet, the cat swayed, in rhythm with the song. Misfortune always comes to an end, ten, twenty, thirty or even forty years, whatever path it took, as long as you respect time. Julia looked at her husband, horrified. Olivier was staring at the animal, which was now on its hind legs.

« Jamais je n'ai abandonné l'espoir,
Certaine, j'ai toujours été de te revoir,
Mon amour d'enfant, ma belle Abigaël,
Dans ces traits bestiaux toujours aussi belle.
[I never gave up hope, I was always sure that I'd
see you again, My darling child, my beautiful
Abigail, Even as an animal, you're still so
beautiful.]
Thick smoke gradually invaded the scene. It was

coming from the cat, which seemed to be getting bigger and bigger.

"Tu nous a donné la force de continuer à croire,
De ne jamais nous abandonner au désespoir,
Enfin, nos retrouvailles nous ont été accordées,
Et tous les trois, seront enfin en paix."
[You gave us the strength to continue to believe,
To never give up hope, And finally our reunion has
been granted, And all three of us will live in
peace."]

An explosion rang out on these last words. Instinctively protecting themselves, Julia and Olivier dropped down, protecting themselves with their arms. On the stage, next to Betty and Tony, a little girl was sobbing.

Next to her was a cat with fur as black as ebony and blue eyes, as blue as water in a lake, looking right and left, as if it were lost.

Everyone in the theater stood up and applauded.

*

When she had finished eating, Andrea went to the restrooms while her husband was paying at the cash register. They were really having nice sunny weather. They were lucky. It was only the beginning of April and having such nice weather in this part of France was far from being guaranteed. The Easter week-end was an opportunity for the Merrin family to take a short break. Even at

Christmas, it had been impossible for them to leave the Parisian suburbs. And their daughter Ariel had been on their backs for ages, hounding them so they'd take her to Gévaudan, down in the south of France, where there was a zoo with wolves in it. This long week-end was going to be full of surprises and discoveries and she couldn't wait to get there! In front of the very contemporary bathroom sink in this modern and surprising restaurant, Andrea brushed back her hair and smiled at herself, a radiant smile reflected in this mirror lit up with elegant metallic spotlights. This is a mind-boggling place! she thought to herself. Happy with the way she looked, she headed towards the door, ready to join Pierre and her daughter to hit the road again, when she heard someone behind her ask:

"Excuse me Ma'am. Have you seen my daughter?"

In the parking lot, a black cat was walking towards the woods, its blue eyes looking at a little girl on the slide.

A walk in the woods

Dedication and courage do the job.
Gabriel Meunier (1568)

I personally never believed in ghosts. I've never even been superstitious: I never would have gone out of my way not to go under a ladder or have taken another path just because I saw a black cat in front of me. Nonetheless, I've always liked thrillers or horror films, ones that chill your blood, even though I completely forget them as soon as they're over.

The story I'm about to tell you is something that happened to me, in an ordinary context, on a day just like any other. I'm not asking anyone to believe this, you can do whatever you like with it. Some people I'm sure will say that I'm inventing things, lying, or making things up. But I'm just going to tell you what happened, what happened to me, nothing else. It's up to you...

***

Ever since I was a little girl, I've always

loved horses. Unfortunately, I never had enough money, or to be more exact, my parents never had enough money to buy me one. Despite that, I took riding lessons for years, thus satisfying my equestrian passion. A couple of years ago I was training the horses belonging to a riding champion who lived not too far away. It was a win-win situation, as I exercised his horses when he wasn't available and they were first-rate ones, and so I also made a lot of progress.

It was a nice April morning, back in 1997, early, about seven thirty. Do you remember that this was an unseasonably hot spring that year in Normandy? That's why I preferred to go out nice and early, avoiding the heat for the horses, as well as for myself. I wanted to go for a nice ride to start off the day. I picked out a little chestnut mare called Callisto.

After a quick grooming, I carefully put the tack on: bridle, breastplate and saddle. After quickly adjusting everything, both of us were ready for a run in the woods. Callisto was a lively little mare, always happy and gentle. So she followed me calmly in the narrow hall, her bells tingling to the sound of the rubber. Once I was in the saddle, I let her walk up to the sand on the path that the sun had lit up with its morning beams, letting her stretch her legs, still stiff with sleep, before heading off into the forest.

She swayed her rump as usual, breaking into a brisk trot, letting me know that she was impatient to be leaving the stables. Callisto and I trotted out to the path leading to the gate of the property, which, luckily for me, was open, so I didn't have to get off. I looked right and left, just to make sure no cars were coming, and we set out on the right, towards the forest that we could make out in the distance. It wasn't even eight o'clock, yet I already knew it was going to be a scorcher today.

The picture-perfect blue sky was there to guarantee us a nice hot day. I was being rocked by the mare's rhythm, who was flickering his ears back and forth, in an echo to the sound of the birds chirping. I could feel a hearty intake of breath building itself up under the saddle and Callisto let me know how happy he was to be out by belting out a loud neigh. Two cows grazing in the meadow alongside the road raised their somewhat dull-looking eyes, glancing at us for a moment, before going back to their business in the sweet green grass. When we reached the little bridge over the river, the mare stopped, without being asked to. She apparently appreciated the scenery as much as I did.

This site always made me think of a mountainous landscape, where the shadows from the trees were reflected in the water like a mirror lake. We could hear tiny waves splashing and a refreshing little breeze from the Pyrenees picked up to cool us down: I just loved coming here! We started off again and soon reached the forest.

On the path going through the woods, the beauty of the trees glistening with morning dew made me indescribably happy. All of these huge trees - poplars, birch trees and probably some oaks too (botany was never my favorite subject at school) threw their imposing shadows at our feet.

The mare was still swaying to and froe, just as happy as I was to be out. An orchestra of birds was singing, all busy, I imagined, playing subtle games they only knew the rules to. I could see some bees buzzing from flower to flower, stocking up on huge reserves of pollen. A handful of flies were flying around Callisto's ears, though there weren't enough of them to spoil this beautiful day for us. I was basking in this beginning of a summery day. We soon reached a fork in the path: it went off to the right towards a dark and muddy part of the woods I had never been to, and to the left, it led to a little clearing about three hundred feet away. Of course we took the second option. I urged my mare into a trot. Callisto didn't refuse this, biting down on her bit and looking straight ahead, paying attention to my indications. When we were about halfway there, there was a branch blocking the path, an instead of carefully stepping over it, she sped up and jumped, continuing with a canter. I understood that she didn't feel like sleeping in this morning. She suddenly veered, surprised by a dog leaning against the fence of the house next to the clearing.

Astonished by this reaction, I tried my best to control her. She quickly realized though that she had nothing to worry about and calmed down. I continued down the rest of the path at a peaceful walking pace. This led to a crossing: on the left we would be going back to the main road where we came from, and on the right we would continue our way through the woods. Of course we decided to go through the forest and I urged her to trot again. The dense undergrowth cooled us down and Callisto was attentive to my orders. However, without having ordered her to do this, she started to speed up her pace. My fingers pulled back on the reins, but to no avail. Her ears were down and she kicked up her legs.

I turned around, expecting to see a couple of cyclists, as was often the case, but instead of that, I saw a man dressed in black, looking at us from behind a tree, out of the corner of my eye. I pulled Callisto to a stop, had her turn around and go towards him. Nothing was there. He had vanished. Callisto however, was huffing and puffing and wanted to race off in the opposite direction. I tried to calm her down by petting her on her neck when I heard a noise on my right. I saw a beautiful deer followed by two little fawns in the underbrush.

This seemed crazy. Was I hallucinating? Did I mistake the animal for something else? It must have been an optical illusion caused by all the shadows. I couldn't help but thinking that the animal was on the right side of the path whereas "the man" that I thought I saw was on the left.

I decided to keep going anyway and pushed Callisto into a trot. A few minutes later she had calmed down and was back in sync. I must have been mistaken. But what worried me was Callisto's reaction. How could I explain her fright if this was a mere product of my imagination? Had she just smelled the deer, she wouldn't have reacted like that. We often stumbled across them when we were out riding and she was more curious than afraid. Horses, though, are able to sense fear in their riders, and in this case, perhaps I myself transmitted my fear when I thought I saw this "man." Yes, but I turned around because Callisto had lowered her ears and kicked, meaning that she was the one who had the first reaction, not me. But in the end, no one was there, like the man had vanished into thin air, crazy. I finally concluded, albeit with skepticism, that it must have been a shadow and that my mare was frightened by the presence of the deer. This hypothesis seemed to be the most likely one and I tried to persuade myself that it was the right one.

The path led to a clearing in the middle of two large fields. We had been trotting for about a quarter of an hour now and I decided to give my mare a short rest. That peculiar feeling I had had was now gone, probably because I could see the sun once again and hear the birds singing away. A minute or two after that, we felt as good as we did at the beginning of our ride. The mare was strolling along without hesitation, as she usually did, and her ears were twitching to the sounds of the surrounding countryside. Nothing was going to happen in this neck of the woods. I was on familiar territory, nothing could happen to us here. The mere idea that I could have seen someone hiding behind one of these trees suddenly seemed ridiculous to me. I actually burst out laughing, thinking of my exaggerated apprehension a while ago. I even thought of this guy running after me: what would his chances to catch up to me have been? None. Me, horseback riding, him on foot, or even had he been in a car or riding a bike, I would have been much faster. There's no way he could have caught up to my horse in these woods.

My mare suddenly stopped dead in her tracks. I was violently pushed forward. My nose slammed into her neck, causing a sudden and intense pain. I raised a hand to my face, and felt a warm liquid running down. I was bleeding. Callisto still wasn't moving, but I didn't even notice this. Muttering a few words under my breath to her, I scrounged around for a Kleenex that should logically be in one of my pockets. I dug my heels in so she'd start walking again. I didn't even notice that she wasn't paying any attention to my orders, too busy trying to stem this bloody river rolling down my face. I finally found a piece of tissue paper and raised to to my nose, while looking up. I didn't see anything that shouldn't have been there.

Callisto was standing straight as a post, her ears pointing forward and her nostrils dilated. She was breathing heavily and I could feel her stomach swelling under the saddle. She was trying to figure out why she was so frightened. As I had no idea myself, I automatically looked in the same direction as she was. About a hundred and fifty feet in front of me, leading into the second part of the forest, I made out a shadow right on the other side of the path. The mare pivoted and wanted to flee. My Kleenex fell out of my hand when I was trying to control her, and turning around, she stomped on it. I luckily wasn't bleeding any more, though my nose was still throbbing. I pulled the mare back so she was facing the forest again. Then I saw him distinctly, for the first time. He had moved to the middle of the path. The "man" was wearing very long black trousers, so long that I couldn't even see his feet. His head was leaning down, and I couldn't even make out his traits on his face. His skull was covered with some sort of hood attached to a blackish tunic. I had only been looking at him for no more than four or five seconds but I was already completely panicked. This man had followed me. How could he have gone in front of me without me noticing him, because I'm sure he was the same guy I had seen before. Had he heard me laugh, and was he gloating over my lack of vigilance?   And how could he have known that I'd be going towards the second part of the forest? Like did that mean he knew where I usually went riding? If so, perhaps he had been stalking me for the past few days now.

Callisto started to piaffe and turned sharply around once again. She wanted to bolt away with a gallop, but I was able to stop her for a few moments. I was facing the forest, once again, but once again, nothing was there. Neither on the path nor in the undergrowth. No way was I going to think of this mysterious shadow and no way was I going to take this path again. The mare was still restless. We turned around and she started trotting. Despite my apprehension and desire to get back to the stables as soon as possible, I made her slow down to a walk. If I had let her speed up, I'm sure she would have broken out into a gallop and her panic, added to my own, wouldn't have been good for either of us. What could I have done had she gone out of control? What if I fell off? I turned around to make sure this "person", or whatever, was no longer here. No one. After we'd been walking for a minute or so, I heard a rubbing nose. I bent forward, leaning on Callisto's neck, and saw what I had feared: one of her gaiters was almost falling off, and to top everything, my nose had started to bleed again. I had no other choice than to attach this protective element again. I really didn't want to leave my comforting and comfortable saddle (just thinking about this though I took the bottom of my tee-shirt to wipe away the blood that was no longer trickling out of my nose), but anyway, if we had to make a run for it, I didn't want Callisto to trip over this semi-attached gaiter and fall over, with me riding her! I didn't know what to do. This or that? I had to make up my mind quickly: get off and get back on the horse quickly or stay in the saddle and risking have Callisto trip and fall.

The vision of the mare on the ground, trying to get up with a broken leg, and me, certainly injured too, was the trigger. I turned around again, nothing in view. I stopped Callisto; she was nervous. She stepped forward. I pulled the reins back. She stopped, her ears straight up, looking right and left. Right when I was ready to get off, she started walking again. Once again I stopped her. She had to trust me, listen to my orders. I kept a tight hold on the reins, forcing myself to count to five, very slowly. She stood still. I loosened my grip slightly, giving the bridle an inch or two of leeway. She was still paying attention to her surroundings but was no longer trying to walk away. I rubbed her neck, trying both to soothe and encourage her. This had to be done quickly. Once I had gotten off, I'd have to pass the reins over her neck so that I'd still have them in my hands, making me loose a few more seconds. Callisto was immobile. I'd have to hurry.

A noise on the right made us both turn our

heads at the same time. Something was moving in the underbrush, about fifty feet away. Was he lying on the ground, spying on us? Impossible, I would have seen him, I said to myself, in a type of self-persuasion. I was facing the sun and it was shining brightly so I squinted my eyes and put one of my hands like a visor, trying to see where the noise had come from. The mare was the first one to see that we weren't in danger. A few seconds later, I saw the deer that we had seen earlier suddenly get up, immediately followed by her two fawns. Something had scared her: was it us or him? Callisto had moved her head and seemed to have calmed down. On the other hand, I realized that I had been holding on to the reins so tightly that my fingers hurt. I loosened my grip up slightly and the mare lowered her head to munch on a tuft of grass. It was now or never, if she had calmed down it meant she wasn't in any danger, and if she wasn't in any danger, neither was I. I took my feet out of the stirrups and raised my leg over her rump, but with so much conviction that she jumped sideways. I lost my balance and ended up on my knees on the ground. Luckily, as I was an experienced rider, I kept my hands tight on the reins, which prevented her from running off.

I had ripped my trousers and scraped my leg during my fall. Miraculously though, my nose hadn't started bleeding again, but my elbow was grazed by the rocky ground. I could feel tears starting to dwell up and they quickly ran down my face. My right hand started to tremble and I panicked, afraid of something, but what? I felt nauseous, bile rising in my throat, and I had to make a superhuman effort to quell it. The mare was astonishingly calm. Tears were now streaming down my cheeks and I was finding it hard to breathe. Callisto then placed the tip of her muzzle against my chest. The roles were now inversed. I was overcome by a sense of extreme weariness and fatigue. It must have been the combination of fear, being annoyed and that terrible heat. I took it on myself and forced myself to close my eyes for a few seconds and breathe slowly. I was counting on Callisto to warn me of any danger. Once I had finished this little yoga session, my fear had not disappeared, but I had calmed down a bit. I got up slowly so that I wouldn't frighten her as I did just a few minutes ago. I looked around and saw that the gaiter had come loose during all of this and that it had been thrown off about fifteen feet away. I'd have to go get it.

I took a step forward, expecting Callisto to follow me, but she wouldn't budge. I turned to look at her, astonished, clucking my tongue to encourage her. Not a step. She remained as still as a statue, her four feet planted into the soil. "Come on," I said, trying to persuade her. Just hearing my voice I realized how distraught I was, ready to burst into tears once again. She finally decided to get going and took one step ahead, then two and then three and stopped, sniffing the air, ears perked and eyes worried. I never even thought about just leaving that gaiter where it was and hightailing it out. I still don't know why. My certainly flawed logic was telling me that I absolutely had to get that gaiter back and I couldn't leave it where it was. Or at least not yet.

We'd advanced about halfway of the distance separating us from our goal. I tried to continue, but once again, Callisto refused to budge. I was starting to get seriously annoyed, which of course was not the type of behavior to have around a horse. "Get going!" I shouted again, but his time she stepped backwards. At the price of a huge effort causing my bottom lip to start bleeding, I stemmed my tears. I didn't move, concentrating on the ocular dam that I had to close. That was when I noticed the deer in the undergrowth, about twenty or twenty-five feet from us. This time she was really close. She was alone, her fawns weren't there. She was lying down, resting underneath the trees.

Then I noticed something strange: flies, dozens of flies were flying above the animal. In fact, they formed a huge black cloud around her body, going from one place to another in a very precisely choreographed ballet: from her head to her stomach, from her head to... I lowered my eyes and discovered a gaping hole in her abdomen. There were blood stains on her beautiful formerly white fur. How could I have thought she was sleeping? And her look... black, even more frightening as her eyes were empty, stripped of any expression. A horrible feeling of nausea came over me. I was about to vomit. My head started to spin when I realized what I was looking at: the vision of the deer's cadaver, the deafening buzz of the flies and the temperature that had shot up several degrees in the past few seconds.

My hair was glued to the nape of my neck, my cheeks, my forehead. Sweat was running down my body and blood was once again flowing out of my nose. A pestilential stench of rotted flesh tickled my nostrils. I just had enough time to lean forward and threw up everything I had in my stomach. One hand was holding my hair back, the other was holding on to Callisto's left rein, my fingers whitened and cramped. For a long time I remained like that, folded in half, head down, drops of blood making a puddle at my feet. When I was able to raise my head again, everything around me started spinning and I fell to my knees, my right hand still holding on to one of the reins, trying to catch my breath. I tried to calm down, and when I thought I finally had, tried to get up. I stood up and without warning, was hit by a second round of nausea. I threw up again, this time kneeling in the grass, letting go of the reins that linked me to the mare.

Panicked, I tried to get ahold of the lost rein by groping around behind me. I felt a neck and understood that Callisto was next to me, touching me with her muzzle. I turned around and sat in the grass with an irrepressible desire just to lie down and wait for some passerby to come and take me home. There are usually lots of athletes on this path: bikers, joggers, and people just walking or riding their horses. But today I hadn't seen a soul, and probably wouldn't either. The mare snuggled her head up to me again and this time the dam that I was trying so hard to hold back opened up all of a sudden. A river of tears spilled out, combined with sob, hiccups and spasms. I wanted to get up, but my legs wouldn't support me, all of my force had abandoned me. I couldn't stand up. I tried again and sat right down. My stomach was gurgling, but I succeeded in ignoring it. The tips of my tennis shoes were spattered with blood, just like the bottom of my tee-shirt and my pants were ripped. If anyone were to happen by, what would their reaction be when they saw me? I raised a hand to my face. It was like my nose had doubled in volume, just like my bottom lip. What a sight for sorry eyes I must have been. Only God must have known. And the man hidden somewhere in the forest.

What kind of person could have done that to the deer, as I was persuaded that it was him? He was out there, in the woods, observing me and drooling over the spectacle that I must have been giving him. This idea brought me the courage I needed to get back up. I did so, though it was not easy, leaning on my horse. I saw her gaiter in the underbrush, but decided to leave it there.

I had to get back up into the saddle. I hoisted myself back up, holding on to her mane. We turned around and I decided to go back on the right hand path that led to the road. Not a lot of people used this one, but I'd feel much safer than going through the woods. The mare was serene. I'd always wonder what she could have imagined that day. I was distraught, terrorized, so frightened that I was holding onto her mane, and she was just walking along as if nothing had happened. When we reached the main trail, I decided to speed up to a trot. We had to get back as quickly as possible. I couldn't bear it here anymore. I hated this forest. Every little shadow, every little noise was a source of doubt. Even the cutie little birdies had become unbearable squawkers. The cool temperatures in the undergrowth, which had seemed so pleasant at the beginning of our ride, were now making me shiver. Now I was looking for some sun to reassure myself. The mare didn't want to trot. I urged her on once again, but she slowed down. I kicked her, but she didn't respond, and stopped. "Get going! I want to get out of here!" I whined. Now she was backing up. The more I kicked her the more she backed up. She started to piaffe and with a loud neigh shattered the silence.

At the end of the road, right at the beginning of the path, the man in black was there. He was kneeling down, his hands together as if he was praying, his head and shoulders bent towards the ground. When I saw this I think my brain stopped functioning. The only thing I could think about what my own terror. I remember that I told myself to hold on to her mane and never ever let go. The mare turned her back to him, starting to gallop down the trail in the opposite direction. I was holding on for dear life; all I could think of was not falling off. I entrusted my life to Callisto. I had totally lost control of my horse, the only thing I could hope for is that she'd be heading back to the stables. We quickly got to the fork in the trail. I had to get ready to shift from one side or the other. If my body didn't follow hers, I'd inevitably be thrown off. I chose the right, and the mare turned... to the right, towards the stables! Dust was coming up off her hooves, and pebbles were flying out in all directions. Her hooves were hammering down on the ground and whitish froth was flowing out of her mouth, sticking on her chest. The other part of the forest was coming up almost on the horizon, at the end of that long straight line that we still had to go. She was still galloping as fast as she could and I was being shaken up and bouncing all over. My legs had lost all of their strength and I couldn't find my balance any more, though this had never been a problem for me before.

Then all of a sudden he was here. He appeared before us, on the fringe of the forest. First as an imprecisely shaped shadow, then the black hood, pants and his arms stretched towards the sky. He kneeled down, as if he were praying again. I desperately tried to stop my horse, pulling back as hard as I could on the reins. She lowered her head so I'd let go, which unbalanced me. I hung to her neck for dear life. Callisto was still running straight to the Thing, without slowing down, without the least hesitation in her gate. The two fawns then appeared on each side of the monster, blithely jumping up and down around him. He grabbed one of them with his hands and plunged his head into its abdomen, ripping its guts out. We heard a heart-rendering cry. This scene seemed like it would never end. He then threw the little animal's body into the undergrowth and did the same thing with the second fawn, after having licked up the hot liquid pouring out of its wound.

We'd arrived at the Thing that was now stretching out his arms towards us. I just had the time to make out his hands: long, pale and skeletal. Speeding towards it, Callisto adjusted her gate and jumped high above it. I let out a never-ending scream. When we landed, the mare lashed out with her heels, but luckily I wasn't thrown off. She turned left and we were back in the little clearing. When the dog saw us, he ran to the fence, barking. The mare didn't even look at him and kept on going. She jumped over the branch that we'd seen in the middle of the path just a while ago. She was huffing and puffing, visibly out of strength. She started trotting when we got to the road. Only then was I able to get this situation back under control. I motioned her to start walking, which she did immediately. My whole body shivered when we were going over the little bridge that seemed to peaceful to me before. The forest in back now terrified me. The cows looked up to us, as stoically as they had before. The gate had remained open and we went into the yard. I got off in front of the stables and unsaddled Callisto. Sweat was running down her. It took the hose and turned it towards the mare before turning it on myself, letting the cold water run from my hair and down my back.

I finally put my horse back in her box. I squatted down in a corner and she put her head on my shoulder. I started crying, this time from relief. I slowly got up and walked out of the stables. I got a halter and put it on her. I let Callisto out into the prairie next to the stables and looked at her for a few seconds. After having bucked once or twice and sprinted up and down, she calmed down and started grazing peacefully. Looking at her, all I could do is to thank her for saving my life. She was brave enough to confront him - confront it, should I say. This was an adventure neither of us could ever forget.

*

For a while I continued riding this cavalier's horses. But of course, I never went back into that forest. One of the girls who also worked in these stables told me she thought someone had been following her. But she never saw anything. Never saw anyone. I just answered that I'd also had this strange impression. Whatever, after that I always rode Callisto and the other horses on a trail called "The Ridges," overlooking the Seine River, a place with no trees at all and one, in my opinion anyway, where there was no danger.

Thank God, I never saw him again.

Now I don't ride much anymore, I'm working too much. I however often see Callisto on TV in horse shows. She's become an incredible champion and has won quite a few trophies. The courage she has when jumping over bars, even the highest and most difficult obstacles, makes all the *aficionados* admire her. But I had personally experienced how brave she was, and I'll never forget that because of it, she was the one who kept us both alive on this beautiful spring morning in April 1997.

Keep the Closet Closed

I was sitting on the steps outside school with my best friend, Amy. We were looking at this pretentious Kenny McDoil who was winning each round of marbles. A little farther away, Jenny and her band were pretending to be in a fashion catwalk. Amy sighed. I looked at her, raised my eyebrows and said:

"Don't tell me that you want to be a part of their click."

"Well, they look like they're having fun..."

"All a bunch of stuck up showoffs!"

"Yeah..." Amy answered, not really convinced.

I looked at Jenny. She was playing with her hair. Posing for imaginary photographers and lifting up her blue skirt to the rhythm of her fans, clapping their hands. How could Amy want to be like her? It's true that Jenny was pretty with long blond hair and big blue eyes, but Amy was cute too, even though physically she was quite her opposite.

Kenny won his last round of marbles and put his winnings into a pouch he carried just for that. He came and sat down next to us and started counting how many marbles he had won, without paying any attention to us. Amy looked at him strangely and then back at Jenny. She seemed to be lost in her daydreams. I nudged her with my elbow so she'd come back to reality.

"Quit thinking about this stuck up girl, you're ten times better than she is!"

"If you say so, but all the boys in school want to go out with her," Kenny said.

"You take care of your marbles and leave us alone," I answered.

"You just say that because you're jealous. Jenny's got everything that you both don't have!"

"Whatever, but I'm sure she wouldn't go out with a loser like you!" said Amy in retaliation.

"You sure about that?" he said defending himself.

"She doesn't go out with kids who are afraid of witches!"

Kenny blanched before bursting out angrily and asked Amy:

"Who told you that?"

"Everyone knows that you see witches at night and you cry like a little baby because you're afraid to go into your room!"

Kenny clenched his fists. He was so mad he was trembling with rage. He got up quickly, spilling his marble pouch onto the ground. The marbles all rolled all over. He didn't even pay any attention to this and ran to the other side of the schoolyard, certainly looking for the traitor so he'd spill the beans.

"What's this stuff about witches?" I asked Amy.

"Like the whole school is talking about that right

now."

"Not me, I never heard that."

"You're always the last one to know!"

"Well, tell me about it then!"

"What they say is that in Kenny's room there's a witch in his closet at night!" whispered Amy to me, just like she was telling me the scoop of the century.

"Says who?"

"Says everyone... But Kenny doesn't want us to repeat that."

"A witch in his closet," I repeated. "Gimme a break."

"Honest to God! And once she even came out and tried to catch him!"

"Too bad she didn't get him, it would have made our lives easier," I said, laughing.

"That's not even funny. I've got to say this like scares the daylights out of me. Now I stick a chair in front of the closet in my bedroom so that she doesn't come to my house."

"That witch isn't in the closet," I replied, looking at Jenny and her click coming towards us.

Jenny came up to Amy, put her hands on her hands on her hips and asked:

"Amy, you want to come and play catwalk with us?"

Amy looked at me, her eyes begging.

"Go ahead..."

She got up and left the schoolyard. I was all alone then and started picking up Kenny's marbles to put them away in his pouch.

The afternoon went by slowly. It was hot and sticky in the classroom and all I could think about was lying down on some freshly cut grass, in the shade of a tree. As I couldn't do that of course, I asked the teacher for permission to go to the bathroom. It wasn't as hot in the hall. There was a slight breeze coming in through the two hall windows that were open and I could smell someone's freshly cut lawn. Summer was coming up fast and that meant summer vacation. I would have liked to have gone out someplace in the countryside, but it wasn't even three-thirty and I still had to wait for more than an hour before school ended for the day.

I opened the bathroom door and came face to face with Kenny, standing at the sinks. I gasped, surprised, when I saw him, thinking that I'd be the only one in there. I let go of the handle and went to the second sink, next to him. I pressed down on the tap and the water came pouring out. I splashed the cool water on my face and arms, appreciating how good it felt.

"You tell anyone, you're dead," Kenny whispered to me.

"What?"

"You heard me. You or your friend, you repeat that and I'll kill both of you."

"There's nothing to be ashamed of, everyone has nightmares sometimes," I answered, a bit more ironically perhaps than I should have.

Without me expecting this, Kenny slapped me on the face so hard that I almost fell down. I caught myself at the last moment on the bathroom sink and succeeded in not falling down onto the tiled floor. I raised my hand to my cheek, looking at Kenny, amazed at what he had done. He didn't budge an inch.

"One more word about that and it's not just a slap on the cheek that you're going to get!"

Kenny disappeared just as fast as his slap on the cheek had arrived. My hand was still on my cheek, not believing that he could have done something like that. I felt tears welling up on the edges of my lower eyelids, and tried my best to make them go away, not wanting to admit that I had been shocked. I looked into the mirror: my left cheek was bright red. What was my teacher going to say? I couldn't stay forever in the bathroom, waiting for it to go away. I put some more cold water on it, the red mark went away a little bit, but you could still see it. I finally decided to go back to the classroom, dragging my heels in the calm and deserted hall. I stopped in front of the door, looking in through the little window. Mrs. Satterman was explaining some math rule on the blackboard. I tried to slip in as quietly as possible.

"Well, Miss Dyer, you certainly took your time!"

"Excuse me Ma'am." I said, sitting down next to Amy.

"What happened to your cheek?" my friend asked.

"I met Kenny McDoil in the bathroom."

"So what happened?"

"He was really made that you told me about this thing with the witches. He said that if we told anyone else, he'd kill us."

"Well everyone already knows about it anyway."

"And then he slapped me and ran away."

"Miss Dyer and Miss McArthur! Perhaps you both want to stay after school? Be quiet now, both of you!" Mrs. Satterman said, reprimanding us.

We both shut up and looked down into our books, but luckily the bell rang, liberating us.

We both rushed out of class, barely taking the time to put our stuff into our lockers. School was finished for the day and the hall was full of kids running up and down. Amy and I went outside. Near a large oak tree on the other side of the schoolyard, Kenny was waiting. He was looking at us and following us with his eyes while we were going down the steps. Amy pretended she hadn't seen him and so did I. Tom went up to him and they started talking. While we were walking towards them to leave the schoolyard, they both stared at us fiercely. I looked right back at Kenny, promising him with my eyes that this slap wasn't going to go down like that.

"What's he looking at you like that for?" asked Amy.

"Who knows? He's crazy. I didn't even know about all that stuff!"

"Forget him, he's an idiot! And same thing's true for his friend, a bunch of losers in this school!" And we both ran home.

It was about eight-thirty or so when my mom told me to brush my teeth and go to bed. I didn't like to turn off the lights right away and she always let me read in bed until about nine or so. Once I had brushed my teeth and put on my pajamas, I had to select my outfit for the next day. I opened my closet, took out a dark blue jean and a yellow tee-shirt. I also chose my very favorite pair of shoes, Converse tennis shoes that Dad had brought me back from Paris. I closed the door, but still was holding on to the door handle. I looked at my chair at my desk and shook my head. I wasn't going to be like Amy! Believing in witches when you're eleven years old - like I'm not a baby! But I did make sure that the door was closed and went to bed. I only read for about fifteen minutes before my eyes started to shut by themselves. I fell asleep right away and had sweet dreams.

I could feel something was up though when I got to school the next day. There were several different groups of kids together and I could see that everyone was speaking vehemently. I made out Jenny and her little friends on the other side of the schoolyard. It seemed to me she was crying but she turned around and I couldn't be sure. I finally walked in to the schoolyard, astonished by all this unceasing noise.

I looked around for Amy but didn't see her anywhere. Mrs. Satterman was on the front steps, with Mr. Cleaver, our principle. She was drying her eyes with a tissue.

Mr. Cleaver had his arm around her shoulder, his face was stern and serious. I stopped in the middle of the path, next to the large oak tree where Kenny McDoil had waited for us yesterday after school. I looked around and noticed that quite a few kids were crying, holding on one to another, like they were trying to console themselves. Now I was getting nervous. What could have happened for everyone to be like this?

A car pulled in in front of the school. A young lady got out; she looked like Tom's mom. She ran to the stairs and ran in, immediately followed by Mrs. Satterman and the principle. The bell rang, telling everyone school was starting, but no one paid any attention to it. I was there, in the middle of the schoolyard, looking at people who were crying, their faces crumbled.

"Lola ! I've been looking for you all over!"

It was Amy. I hadn't seen her come up and she literally jumped up on me. She was all excited and totally panicked.

"What happened?"

"Kenny McDoil is dead!"

"What?!"

"Lola, he's dead! He died last night!"

Things started to swirl around me and my heart

started beating so hard in my chest that I could actually hear it. A wave of heat came over me and I had to hang on to my friend so I wouldn't fall over. I finally sat down in the grass and Amy crouched down next to me.

"Lola, are you okay?"

I didn't answer, I didn't even understand what she was saying. I burst into tears, sorry that I'd insulted him yesterday. Amy took me by the shoulders and started crying with me.

"What...?" I succeeded in asking her.

"I don't know, some of the kids say that his parents found him like that in bed this morning."

"Did he have a heart attack?"

"I don't know. I don't even know what that is."

"I don't either, but that's what people say when you really don't know how people died... it's just when your heart stops beating, that's all."

"Yes, but why did Kenny's heart stop beating? People's hearts stop beating when they're old."

    —   "I don't know..."

The principle motioned for all of us to come in. Contrary to the noise before in the school's playground, you could have heard a fly. Mrs. Satterman was walking up and down the classroom, arms crossed. Everyone took a seat at their desks, looking gloomy and despondent. Mrs. Satterman finally spoke up:

"My dear children, you've all learned what happened to our dear friend Kenny. We were given the bad news early this morning, before any of you arrived. We've now contacted all of your parents. Any of you who would like to go home can do so. If you prefer to stay here at school, the teachers and I will give your classes. Do you have any questions?"

"How did Kenny die?"

Logan Matthews was the one who asked this. Everyone looked at him, then at Mrs. Satterman, secretly hoping she'd be able to answer the question. Mrs. Satterman seemed to be expecting this. At first she seemed embarrassed, but she quickly gathered her wits about her.

"Well, his heart just stopped beating, that's all."

"See, I told you so!" I whispered to Amy.

"But why did it stop?" insisted Logan.

"You can be sick without actually knowing you are, and these are things that happen. His heart must have been tired and neither Kenny nor his parents realized this."

Logan remained dubitative of Mrs. Satterman's answer. He opened his mouth as if he wanted to add something, and immediately closed it.

"It's all right Logan, tell me what's bothering you. We have to talk about this."

Logan looked at Mrs. Satterman with a mixture of suspicion and hesitation, but she nodded her head in encouragement.

"Well, when we were still outside... Some of the kids said that his parents found him with his mouth wide open... Wide open like he was screaming, or like he was terrified of something when he died."

"Who told you that?" asked Mrs. Satterman, severely.

"Um, well Jenny Maland, but she said that Tom Dillinger told her..."

Logan was looking down at his shoes. He was sorry now that he'd spoken up.

"That's a lie! I don't want to hear any of you, not even one single person, say such foolish things! Gossiping about things like this when one of your classmates has just died, how can you? Do you all understand me?"

A chorus of "Yes, Mrs. Satterman" could be heard in the classroom. I looked out the window onto the lawn, Tom's mom was leaving the building with Tom. They both got into the car, slammed the doors and left.

Like they had for all the other parents, the school had contacted my mom to tell her about Kenny's death. She wanted to come and get me, but as Amy's parents both worked, she had to stay at school and I wanted to be with her.

There were only about fifteen of us in class, a little more than half, and Mrs. Satterman went back to her math lesson. It wasn't hard and the others wouldn't have any problems catching up. Everyone was trying to concentrate on what she was saying, but you could tell they were thinking of something else. I was thinking of Kenny. Why did it bother him so much that Amy talked about those witches? That certainly didn't deserve a slap in the face! Even if it was a little babyish, but after all we were only eleven, and not grown-ups...

      The lunch bell finally rang, Amy went to the cafeteria. We sat down and unwrapped our sandwiches. To be honest though, neither of us felt like eating. I nibbled on my meal and opened my can of fruit juice, poking a straw into it. Amy didn't say anything, she was looking at Jenny and her friends coming towards our table. I was really hoping they wouldn't come and bother us, but this was a hope not to be alas, and they sat down next to us and started talking about Kenny.

      I didn't even look at them however it was impossible for me not to hear them. I motioned to Amy to leave, but she wanted to hear what the girls were talking about.

"And we'll never see him again," said Jenny, with a sniffle.

"And he was in love with you," added Lisa, shaking her dark brown hair.

Then they took out their sandwiches and started gobbling them down with their usual grace and distinction.

"Well at least it didn't take their appetites away," I whispered to Amy.

Amy looked at me severely as if she was afraid that one of them could have heard my reflection. But what in the heck did she expect from those three girls?

"Is it true what they say?" asked Mary to Jenny. "That he died of fright?"

"I can't tell you that."

"Come on, please," begged Lisa. "We're your two best friends... Tell us what Tom told you."

"I'm sorry, I can't. I promised Tom I wouldn't say anything."

"Well, if you promised Tom, why did you tell Logan Matthews then?" Those words flew out of my mouth before I realized it. This time if Amy had had a machine gun instead of her eyes, she would have shot me down right there.

"What?" shouted Jenny, turning to look at me.

"You told Logan, didn't you? He told us that in the math course."

"You told Logan and you didn't even tell your best friends?" asked Lisa, her feelings hurt.

"All that because you had a crush on him... everyone knew that anyway," Mary added.

Jenny's mouth dropped open and I could even see a piece of bread she hadn't yet swallowed. Her big blue eyes shifted from Mary towards Lisa and then me. I started slowly nibbling on my chicken sandwich again so I wouldn't have to look at her. I didn't feel like talking to her at all.

"Come on Jenny, you have to tell us what you know. You can't tell Logan and then not tell us!"

Jenny took a big breath. She took a paper napkin and wiped off a side of her mouth where there was some mayonnaise. She put her sandwich down again on the table, took a sip of Coca-Cola Light and looked at her friends, imploring them.

"You have to promise me you're not going to tell

anyone!"

"Promise !" answered Mary and Lisa at the same time.

"You too!" she said, speaking to Amy and me.

"Everybody know, I told you that Logan said that in front of the whole class."

"Promise," Amy said again.

Jenny looked at me sternly.

"Promise," I said ironically, rolling my eyes.

"So here you go," Jenny started. "So what happened, at least what Tom told me happened, is that Kenny's parents found him dead in the morning in his bed and you could see by the expression on his face that he was terrified."

"So how did he find out?" asked Mary.

"Kenny's mom phoned Tom's mom. And he heard everything because he said that his mom repeated every single word that Kenny's mom said."

"Yeah but how come Kenny's mom called Tom's mom? Were they friends? Lisa asked.

"They were BFF, that's why Kenny and Tom were always together."

I was sick and tired of hearing all of this crap so I butted in:

"Mrs. Satterman told us that all that wasn't true and Kenny was sick, that's why he died. You guys just say anything at all!"

"But it was true," insisted Jenny. "And Tom even said that the wicked witch came to get him!"

Everyone shut up and looked at Jenny strangely, waiting for more.

"What?! What are you all looking at me like that for?"

"Cause you said a witch got Kenny and killed him!" I couldn't help laughing this was so ridiculous.

"Tom saw it. He saw the witch."

"He saw the witch?" repeated Lisa.

"That was what I wasn't supposed to tell anyone. But anyway, here goes. He slept over at Kenny's once. He didn't want to believe Kenny about this witch coming out of his closet at night. But he saw it with his own eyes and it scared the liver out of him. That's why he's convinced that Kenny died of fright last night when the witch came to get him."

Jenny was so sincere saying this that it made me uncomfortable. I started doubting what Mrs. Satterman had said. Maybe Kenny wasn't really sick after all? Maybe he had seen the witch last night? Maybe she came to get him to take his soul with her? I shivered and Amy asked me if I was okay. I nodded my head, got up, picked up my sandwich wrappings and left our lunch table. I left Amy with Jenny and her friends; I wanted to be alone. I sat down underneath the big oak tree, my head leaning against its rough bark and finally let my tears start falling. This didn't make any sense. Why would God let a child die?

The one o'clock bell rang, telling us the day wasn't over yet. Amy must have left the lunch table with the other girls because I didn't see her. It was no big deal, I'd see her again in class. I got up, brushed the grass off of my rear, picked up my back-pack and went up the little slope leading to the steps. I went into the hall. Most of the students were already in their classrooms, as I had lagged behind a bit. I was in front of the teacher's room and stopped when I heard Mrs. Satterman's voice. The door was slightly ajar, and I could hear what she was saying to Mr. Cleaver. I put my ear to the wall.

"... always been a good student."

"I heard there's going to be an autopsy to see what he actually died from..." Cleaver continued.

"Poor kid... And his parents... Not knowing why the Lord took your child away... It's frightful."

"Calm down, Louisa. I know this is sad but you have your students to think about. You have to pull yourself together, they all need you."

"I know, you're right, my students are waiting for me. I have to be there for them," she said, sniffing. "But it's horrible, it's horrible... And the rumor about his face being distorted by fear is already circulating; one of the students asked me the question..."

"None of the children should know about that: that could spread panic through the whole school."

"I have to go now Mr. Cleaver, I'm sure they're already in class."

"Okay, Louisa, you can do it. Don't forget that you're a model for them."

"You're right, Mr. Cleave."

I ran to the classroom as fast as I could so Mrs. Satterman wouldn't see me out in the hall. I arrived at the door out of breath and went in, as calmly as I could. I sat down at my desk; Amy was already there.

"What's up, you look pretty strange?" she asked.

"It was true..."

"What was true?"

"What Jenny told us about Kenny... that he died of fear."

"How do you know?"

"I overheard Mrs. Satterman talking to Mr. Cleaver. They said that they didn't want us kids to know this..."

I was talking quickly, half excited and half panicked about what I had just learned. Amy didn't believe what she was hearing either, but she remained calm, or at least she looked like she was.

"We have to talk to Tom," she repeated.

"He left, I saw his mom come and get him."

"No, he came back, I saw him before going in the classroom. He said he didn't want to stay home. We have to ask him if it's true that he saw the witch."

"But Jenny wasn't supposed to tell us that."

"Maybe we can ask her to come with us, and that way, he might tell us if she's with us."

"We have to talk to Jenny during recess and explain this, but I'd prefer it if her friends didn't know anything about this."

"Don't worry! If she tells them not to come, they

won't. They obey her without even thinking."

Mrs. Satterman came into the classroom and we all stopped talking. I took out my workbook like she asked us to do and tried, without succeeding very well I must say, to concentrate on square roots. It felt like all we were doing was math, and believe me, that was something that sucked.

As I was looking at my paper on my desk, trying to find the correct answer, I didn't see Mrs. Satterman come up to Bryan Palmec.

"What's this?" she asked, snatching the piece of paper from his hands. Did Mr. Matthews give you this message?

"Umm, no I was just passing it..."

« Ah ! All right then. So what does this Very Important Message say then?" she asked, unfolding it.

I saw her face fall apart reading it. Her face had turned red with rage and she started to tremble. Her big green eyes started to shrink behind her glasses and she shouted:

"Who wrote this?"

No one answered: everyone lowered their eyes towards the mathematical formulas and no one said a word.

"I'm asking you this one more time: who wrote all of this nonsense?"

Still no answer.

"So! As the guilty person is a coward who's afraid of assuming his acts, I'm giving a test to the whole class!

This brought on a rumor of protestation, but Mrs. Satterman quelled that immediately.

"And I don't want to hear another word or you'll all be staying after school for two hours!"

At the end of the class, Amy and I cornered Logan:

"What was on that note?" I asked.

Logan wanted to leave, but I was holding on to his sweatshirt hood. Mrs. Satterman, who could see us from the classroom, scrunched up her eyes. I dragged Logan to the wall and whispered, holding on to him tightly:

"Logan, tell us what was written on that note!"

"I can't, they're going to yell at me again."

"Don't worry, we won't tell anyone that you're the one who told us, we'll say that we saw it when Mrs. Satterman read it, okay?"

Logan looked at both of us, suspiciously.

"You swear it?"

"Cross my heart and hope to die," I answered, impatiently.

"Tom saw the witch in his closet too."

I let go of Logan's arm and he ran off. I remained with Amy, who look at me, astonished.

"We have to find Tom," I said.

"Jenny first," she answered. "We'll have more luck with Jenny."

"You're right, let's go."

When we got to the steps, Amy and I saw Jenny coming in through the front gate, alone. We ran towards her, running down the stairs and onto the lawn just like two sprinters.

"Jenny ! Wait for us!" I shouted.

She turned around and stopped so we could catch up. She looked strange though and seemed nervous.

"What's wrong?" asked Amy.

"Nothing."

"You're not with Mary and Lisa?"

"No, I'm going home."

And she turned around.

"Jenny ! Wait a second, Amy and I have a question for you."

"Now what do you want?" she asked, continuing to walk.

"We want to go see Tom. But we want you to come with us."

"How come? What do you want with Tom?"

"To know if he actually did see the witch."

"You promised me you wouldn't say anything!" she exploded.

"There's a note going around... apparently other kids know about this. We just wanted to ask Tom if this was true and we thought that if you were there, he'd be more willing to tell us..."

"Leave me alone!" And she ran off.

Amy and I looked at her running away, wondering what the heck she had.

"What's wrong with her?" asked Amy.

"Got me, at noon she seemed fine..."

"Hey look, Mary and Lisa are coming."

"So, what did she say to you?" asked Lisa.

"To leave her alone," I answered. "What's wrong

with her?"

"I don't know," continued Mary, "but we were waiting for her in the hall because she was in the bathroom and she opened the door and ran out like a bat out of hell... She ran right in front of us like we weren't even there."

"That is strange," I answered, almost to myself. "Come on Amy, let's go home."

I left Amy at the intersection and went home. This day had been really strange and exceptionally long. I felt like I had lived two days in one. I was exhausted, emptied out. I only wanted one thing: to go home and talk to my mom. I needed to.

We spent a lot of time together that evening, more than usual. My mom and dad were there for me, consoling me to their best, finding the right and appropriate words, like they always did.

I went up to my bedroom about ten. It was quiet up there; my parents were watching TV downstairs. I closed my bedroom door and sat down on the bed. I picked up my teddy bear and held it tightly. I finally put it back down on the bed and went to my closet to get my clothes out for the next day. As I was about to open the door, I thought I heard a noise. I stopped, listened closely, not even daring to breathe.

A few seconds later, as I didn't hear it again, I was brave enough to take a few steps forward, trying to breathe as lightly as possible. I went to the closet and put my hand out to open the door when the noise repeated itself, lightly but distinctly. It was like someone was scratching at the door from the inside. I stopped again and looked around. My baseball bat was on the chair next to my desk. I picked it up. I returned in front of the door. I was only a few feet away and could almost reach the doorknob. I'd devised a simple plan : I was going to open the closet door and hit what was behind that door as hard as I could. I started to sweat and held on to my arm with all of my strength to keep my hands from trembling. I extended my left hand to reach the doorknob, but I was still too far away. I took a little step forward, my heart was beating just as if it were in a rock concert and I felt like I had the Red Hot Chili Peppers inside of me. My legs were quivering, but I made myself continue forward a bit more. This time I was there, my hand reached the doorknob and just when I was about to open it, I heard another scratching sound, this one much louder, in the otherwise silent room. I let go and backed up a few steps, falling on the bed with surprise. I dropped my baseball bat on the carpet. Completely panicked, I jumped off the bed and grabbed the bat, tumbling onto the floor. I got back up and quickly went to the closet, my bat ready. I put my hand on the doorknob, turned it, yanked the door open and swooshed through the air with my formidable weapon.

I swung it so hard that the force of my attack made me spin. My legs got tangled up and the bat hit the wall. A piece of plaster fell off. I found myself on the floor, facing Squeeky, the neighbor's cat.

"Meow" he said to me.

I don't know if that meow was to thank me for busting him out of his prison or to tell me I was completely crazy to be defending myself like that for a simple alley cat.

He jumped onto my desk and went out of my open window.

"Lola !" shouted my mom from downstairs. "What's going on up there? Are you okay?"

"I'm fine mom."

I got back up, dazed by the fright I had just had. I had hurt my arm swinging that batt so hard. My baseball coach would have been proud of me had he been there! I put my formidable weapon back down on a chair and opened the closet. I went in and turned on the light. Everything was nice and tidy where it should have been and smelled like fabric softener. I took out an outfit for the next day, went out and pushed a chair up against the door. I looked at it for a second and to make sure, added a little wooden table. Now that I was sure that no one could get in or out, I went to bed and turned off the lights.

My night was full of sinister and strange dreams. I dreamed of Kenny. I was with him in the school's restrooms; he was extending his hand out to me in a never-ending death rattle. I could neither shout nor move. I was looking at my feet that no longer obeyed me. The ground I was walking on was muddy and sticky. I was sucked into it and couldn't move. I lifted up my feet but the mud held on to my shoes, as if I had walked in hot tar. Kenny was still coming towards me, his arms out like a zombie and his face distorted by torment. He was waiting for me, he was near me. I saw Mrs. Satterman behind him and she said to me:

"Miss Dyer, leave your friends to rest in peace and go back to the classroom. Right now! Or you'll be staying after school with the others!"

She then opened one of the bathroom stall doors. It wasn't a toilet though, rather an enormous hole filled with screaming and dying children. She started laughing, with a shrill laugh that was more like a horse neighing. Kenny wanted to imitate her, but the blood in his throat prevented him and he emitted a grotesque bloody gargle instead.

Both were now coming towards me and I was still stuck in the thick mire running from the taps onto the tiles. Suddenly the walls became liquid and quickly melted, dangerously increasing the level of the sticky silt I would soon be drowning in. Kenny and Mrs. Satterman swallowed and spit out the blackish mud by their noses and mouths in rhythm, both licking their lips on bits of organs half-eaten by vermin. I tried to extricate myself from this sticky trip, but the muck was so thick that my disorderly movements were in vain.

I was awakened by what I thought was the closet door creaking. I got up hastily and turned on my light, but the chair and table were still there. I was sweating and freezing at the same time. The curtains on my window were fluttering with the air coming into my room. I could hear the wind blowing in the birch trees, making our American flag click back and forth. I got up, closed the window and drew the drapes. I went back to bed, looked at the clock - three thirty - had a sip of water and laid back down. I tried to calm myself down by hugging my teddy and turned off the lights a few minutes later.

At the same time, in a small green and white house, a closet door was being deviously opened.

I slept fitfully for the rest of the night. At six, I couldn't stand it anymore so I got up and went to have breakfast. The household was calm. Mom and Dad were still sleeping so I went back upstairs to shower and get dressed. I left for school a little before seven, having left them a note so they wouldn't worry.

I was still focused on my dream. Remembering it made me uneasy. I could still see Kenny and Mrs. Satterman trying to get me and take me into that stinky hole where my friends' doomed erring souls were trapped.

I was in front of Amy's house about seven, but didn't knock on her door.

I got to school a little before seven-thirty, meaning at least half an hour before everyone else. The gate and school were already open, as teachers usually come in early. I walked across the lawn to put my books and my lunch bag in my locker, went up the steps leading to the door and went in. The hall was dark and deserted. The lockers were all identical on both sides of the hall. I reached mine quickly and put my little key in the lock. The slight noise that the little bolt made felt like thunder in this heavy silence and its echo bounced along the walls, yellowed by time and the hands of hundreds of students. I looked around, hoping that no one had heard anything, but apparently I was alone, at least on the ground floor. So I put the lunch that my mom had prepared for me the night before into my locker and was about to put the rest of my stuff in there too, when a little piece of paper caught my eye. I picked it up, turned it over, and read what was written on it:

"Join me as soon as possible in the changing rooms. I have to talk to you."

It was signed Jenny.

Upon reading it, my stomach tightened up with apprehension, once again. I closed my locker door, still holding on to the piece of paper. I quickly went down the hall, opened the doors and ran down the stairs towards the sports field. The sun was starting to shine outside and the birds were chirping in the trees. The morning dew on the grass and little breeze both announced another beautiful day. A perfect day, not too hot, not too cold, you could tell that's what we were going to have. But this horrible feeling that was insinuating itself in me just like a snake slithering through some damp undergrowth in the woods made me dread what was to come.

Jenny was waiting for me on one of the benches in

the changing rooms. She seemed relieved that I'd come. I came in and sat down next to her. Her drawn face proved that she hadn't slept much last night either. Her hair was attached in a ponytail and her bright blue eyes sent out signals of panic.

"What do you want?" I asked her, not even taking time to say hi.

Jenny looked at me and her eyes filled with tears. She hid her face behind one of her hands and mumbled something I couldn't make out.

"I didn't hear what you said," I told her, coming closer.

"Tom's dead!" she sobbed, looking at me. "He's dead! I saw everything this morning!"

"Wh.. What?"

"I was going past his house to come to school... And there were policeman there and an ambulance... So I hid to see what was going on... and then I saw them take Tom out on a stretcher, there was a sheet over him... His mom was screaming and his dad was holding her back so she wouldn't throw herself on the body."

I couldn't believe what I'd heard. I didn't know what to say.

"Lola, he saw the witch! You understand what that means? No one wanted to believe him... He even told his parents about it..."

"You think that...?"

"Of course I do!" she exploded. Kenny saw it and he died and now it's Tom!"

"I had a horrible nightmare last night," I told her.

"I dreamed that Kenny and Mrs. Satterman wanted to take me and throw me into a hole full of other kids... You were there, so was Tom and Amy. I didn't know the other kids. We were in the bathroom at school and Kenny was coming towards me to take me, and I woke up and couldn't fall back to sleep."

"You saw Kenny in the bathroom in your dream?"

"Yeah."

"I saw him yesterday. Just before I left. He was there, in the bathroom, and I saw him in the mirror."

My throat tightened up with a horrible bitter taste. A harsh taste throughout my whole body. The taste fear has. The ball rolling around in my stomach increased in size. Like I could feel it pounding against my stomach walls. It was growing and taking over inside me with so much strength and amplitude as a tornado that wreaked havoc over everything in its passage, leaving only chaos and desolation in its wake. Now I understood why Jenny left so quickly and without any explanations last night.

"I don't know what to do Lola, I'm afraid," she sobbed. "I can't even tell my parents, they'd never believe me."

"We have to find out who saw the witch."

Jenny looked at me and a big tear ran down her cheek, delineating a river bed that would soon become a flood.

"I did... I saw it."

"Oh no..." was all I could say.

"I saw it last night and it's going to come and get me too! I'm afraid, I can't go back home!" Jenny was now crying so hard that her chest was heaving, rising and falling in sharp spasms. I took her by the shoulders and hugged her.

"What am I going to do?" she whispered to herself. "I can't go back to my room."

"What did the witch look like?" I asked.

Jenny looked at me for a second, then raised her eyes so she was looking at the wall, behind me. She didn't say anything at first.

"I didn't know it was the witch right away. I was sleeping, you know. It was the noise that the closet made that woke me up, a creaking noise. I thought I was dreaming, I didn't know it was for real. And there was a breeze in my bedroom. Like I had left the window open. I tried to pull the covers back up over me, but something was holding on to them. And that's what woke me up... And that's when I saw it. The witch was there, at the foot of my bed, squatting. The closet door was open behind her and she was sniggering. She got up and went around the bed so she'd be next to me... I was completely terrorized... I couldn't even call my parents, like I couldn't even make a noise... She pointed her finger towards me and then started laughing, a shrill laugh, I don't know how my parents couldn't hear it..."

I thought back to my dream and how Mrs. Satterman laughed. I started shaking.

Jenny continued:

"And her hair flying around her head, I don't know how, there wasn't any breeze... Her long black hair and her blue eyes that were shining... Lola, I don't know what to do! I don't want her to come, I don't want to die like Kenny and Tom!"

"Come over to my house."

"What? To your house?"

"I can ask my parents if you can sleep over."

"You'd do that for me? Really?"

"Jenny ! If that's what really happens you can't stay at your house."

"But... but I can't stay at your house forever."

"We'll take it one day at a time. For right now I'll ask my mom if you can stay for a couple of days. I'm sure she'll understand that we want to be together seeing what happened to Kenny and Tom."

"And Amy?"

"What about Amy?"

"She's not going to like me going to your house. I mean she really wants to be a part of our group."

"Yeah... But that's not the priority at least not right now."

"You don't like me very much, do you?"

"Um, well let's just say we don't have very much in common."

"Thank you Lola. Thank you for helping me."

I was about to open my mouth and say that she would have done the same thing, that it was normal, blablabla... But I didn't say anything, there was nothing else to say. I accepted her thanks and smiled.

I got up and was about to leave the changing rooms when Jenny asked:

"Lola ?"

I turned around.

"Yeah?"

"Don't say anything... Don't tell anyone what I told you. Not even Amy. I don't want anyone to know about this."

"Okay. I'll keep it to myself."

"Thank you Lola."

I left the changing rooms and walked towards the school where a few students were talking at the doors. They were talking about Tom. The news had spread like wildfire. I walked in, expecting to relive the same thing as yesterday, but this time I'd be prepared. And the whole hall was buzzing, I think everyone had at least one Kleenex out. Mrs. Satterman was heading toward Mr. Cleaver who had just come through the gate. They both went into school quickly. I saw Amy with Lisa and Mary at the other end of the schoolyard. Amy looked like she was really hit hard, she was sobbing and Helen Syendy, who had just joined them, was trying to console her.

I looked at the scene unfolding before me, for a few seconds. Nothing had changed since yesterday except for the victim's name. I knew what would happen next. Half of the kids would go back home and the other half would try to occupy their minds on math or geography. But in the back of their minds, each one would be wondering it the next closet door that would be creaking at night would be theirs, and what type of horrible and evil thing would come out of it to spirit them away from their cozy beds.

I turned around and went back into the changing rooms. I was looking for Jenny but she had left.

"Where's Jenny?" I asked Teddy Bosloth.

"I don't know, I think she left."

"Where'd she go?"

"How should I know?"

I rushed out of the building and circled my eyes over the lawn. Jenny had just gone through the iron gate. I ran as fast as I could to catch up with her.

"Jenny, where are you going?"

"I can't stay here, it's too much for me."

"I'll come with you."

"You're not going to school?"

"No, I don't care."

"And Amy?"

"I'll tell her I went home. I'll call her tonight."

"Alright. What do you want to do?"

"Let's go have a cup of hot chocolate at the Deli. We can talk things over there."

We walked into the little diner and sat down in the booth with its big red bench seats. A few people were having breakfast before going to work, filling up on muffins and piping hot coffee. The fragrance of hot coffee and warm pastries did warm my heart

a little and for a few seconds, I actually felt better.
A young red-haired waitress came to our table, and asked crudely, while continuing to chew her gum:
"What do you want girls?"
Jenny looked at me. I didn't look back.
"Hot chocolate for me, "Ma'am.""
"Same thing for me," replied Jenny.
"It's Miss... I'm a little young to be called 'Ma'am.'"
"What kind of skin care cream to you use?" I asked.
She glared at me and walked away.
"So I don't buy it..." I finished the sentence for Jenny.
Jenny tried to smother her laughter with her hand and looked behind the counter.
"I bet she'll be spitting in our hot chocolate."
I took my cell phone out of my pocket. I sent Amy a message so she wouldn't be worried about me not being in class. I told her I'd call her tonight to see if she was okay.
The waitress brought us our hot chocolates without even looking at us and put the bill down on the table.
"What are we going to do?" sighed Jenny, stirring her hot chocolate.
"I have no idea. We're going to start by seeing if you can sleep over at my house and then we'll take it from there."
"You're right. Our parents have to say it's okay though."

"Don't worry about that. They'll agree."

We remained silent for a long time and then Jenny said, almost to herself:

"I can't believe that Kenny and Tom are both dead."

"I know, it's surrealistic. I feel like I'm going to wake up in a little while and then everything will be like it was before."

"Me too," she said, bursting into tears.

"Jenny..."

I put a hand on her shoulder, trying to comfort her. I didn't really know what to do, I barely knew that girl. And though the image I'd had of her did change because of these events, I still had this type of reticence towards Jenny that blocked me from feeling comfortable with her. I knew that I did what I had to do, but it's true, I felt like I had betrayed Amy even though this thought was patently absurd.

My phone rang. It was my mom. She was worried about me because the school had called her to tell her I'd left and inform her about Tom's death at the same time. I reassured her, telling her where I was and with whom and at the same time asked her if Jenny could sleep over. As I had expected, she said no problem and I hung up, telling her that we'd soon be home, after we went to Jenny's house to get some of her stuff.

We left after that. Outside the street was calm and sunny; a few passersby's were walking on the sidewalks or talking to shopkeepers, happy to find someone to listen to their gossip. Everything seemed peaceful. Life seemed normal, like nothing had changed in these two days. I would have liked to have been in their shoes, ignorant of what had just happened. Ignoring Kenny's death and Tom's too. My thoughts were flitting back and forth in my brain, up and down, right and left, to the point where it was impossible for me to think of anything else, even for a single second. The question I was trying to bury as deep as possible kept surfacing, despite my efforts to keep it down. Just as clear as mountain spring water. It had become an evidence that I had refused to see: where was my name on the list?

After we picked up Jenny's stuff from her house, we went directly home. Jenny couldn't bear to spend any time in her room because the atmosphere there was still full of the witch's presence. I stealthy glanced at the foot of the bed and thought I could see the traces she left last night. For the first time ever since this terrible story began, I could physically feel the evil surrounding us. We only stayed in her room for a couple of minutes but that was long enough for me to feel the evil that it held. The air was heavy and loaded. Like we could almost feel it pushing down on our shoulders. Neither Jenny nor I said a word, each one aware of the other's uneasiness. We didn't need any words though, we just had to leave the room as soon as possible.

Tension had been increasing little by little

throughout the day. Jenny hardly said a word, undoubtedly thinking of tonight, trembling at the idea that the witch would come to get her in my bedroom too. At the dinner table, my parents naturally believed we didn't say a word because we were both traumatized by the death of our classmates. Even when Amy called, I couldn't talk to her, my best friend. My mom excused me, saying that I had already gone to bed and that I'd be at school the following morning.

We were lying next to each other in my double bed. The bedroom ceiling was lit up by moonlight; shadows from the trees in our yard were dancing on it. Jenny and I looked at them, not speaking, watching all the different constantly changing shapes. At the tiniest noise, our hearts stopped beating and our breath remained suspended in the air. Outside a cat meowed its despair so loudly that Jenny grabbed my hand, squeezing it so hard it hurt. My throat was dry, but it was too much bother to take a drink from the glass of water on my bedside table.

Light from the hall passed underneath the door, its weak halo lighting up the closet. Without even looking at her, I knew that Jenny was looking at the doorknob on the closet.

She was dreading the moment where she'd see it turning, where she'd hear the poorly oiled hinges on the doors creak, where a bluish light would take over our room, announcing the witch. I thought of Kenny and Tom. They must have been thinking the same things. They must have experienced the terror of darkness in their rooms. Eyes wide open and attentive to the tiniest suspicious noise while their parents were carrying on with their everyday activities in the neighboring rooms. Alone in their beds, I'm sure they both tried to snuggle up under the useless protection of their covers, paralyzed as I was, unable to even move one hand outside. The wind outside made the tree tap its branches against my window and I would have given anything I had to stop this horrible noise that made me think that someone was softly knocking on my window, asking to come in.

It was freezing cold in my room. I hunkered down as far as possible into the sheets, seeking the warmth and comfort of their cotton. It was twelve forty on my clock. I could hear Jenny breathing. Calm and regular breathing. She had loosened her grip on my hand, and I was sure she had fallen asleep. Lying in my bed, not daring to breathe nor move, I was living the most terrifying night of my existence as a little girl.

I suddenly woke up. I was covered with sweat and freezing. My covers were on the floor. I sat up, put my arm out and grabbed them as quickly as I could. The clock now said three ten. There was no longer any light coming in from under the door; my parents had gone to bed a long time ago. Jenny was still sleeping soundly next to me.

Outside the wind was no longer blowing and the branches were still. Everything was peaceful.

Nothing was moving in the house. I tried to persuade myself that I had no reason to be afraid. I finally turned to the side, pulled my feet up under me, wrapped myself up in the sheets and put my head under the covers. Even if everything seemed to be okay, I didn't want to risk hiding at the bottom of the bed. I finally fell asleep, a restless sleep interrupted by peculiar and disturbing dreams. I dreamed we were at school, all sitting down at our desks. Jenny was in front of me and though I didn't turn around to look at her, I knew that Amy was behind. Mrs. Satterman was talking and each student was carefully writing down the key points. The problem was that she wasn't speaking loud enough. I couldn't hear a thing even though I was trying to understand. I could see her lips moving, but there were no sounds coming out of her mouth, or at least nothing that I could hear. I couldn't note anything at all. What would I do if we had a test? I couldn't learn anything. My stomach twisted with apprehension. I looked at all of my classmates, they were writing things down, taking notes, some of them writing so fast they made holes in their notebooks. Mrs. Satterman was speaking faster and faster; now I could make out some of the words she said, but they didn't make any sense, they weren't coherent sentences. Now she was doing more than just speaking, she was moving, waving her arms, walking up and down the classroom. Jenny was taking notes, taking notes while waving her arms too. She shook her head, tipped it back. Her entire body seemed to be invaded by uncontrollable spasms. I looked at her, stupefied. My pen fell out of my hand, dropping to the ground. A hand touched my thigh, making me almost jump out of my chair. Amy was there, down on her hands and knees, nicely proffering me my pen. I stared at her, horrified. Her face was all puffed up, her bottom lip had been ripped apart, revealing a blackish jaw from which a white worm was wiggling. Her right eye was missing, blood had coagulated in the orbit.

I woke up screaming. Or at least I thought I did. No one was stirring in the house, everyone was still sleeping. I could see the sunrise from my window. I looked at my clock: six a.m. Jenny was still lying next to me. I think she had a good night's sleep which was certainly not my case. I sat up and decided to go downstairs to the kitchen. I couldn't stay in bed any longer. I put on my jean and tee-shirt, trying not to make any noise, put on my tennis shoes and closed the door slowly behind me.

I prepared a hot chocolate for Jenny and I and put some bread in the toaster. The sun was rising and the room was slowly being lit up. I found that comforting. My nightmare had left a bitter taste in my mouth and I was anxious to see Amy and make sure she was okay. I glanced out of the window. The dew on the grass made me think that thousands of diamonds had been deposited on each blade. I saw Squeeky, the neighbor's cat, run by into his house through the cat flap. An ordinary view for an ordinary life, I thought to myself. The bread popped out of the toaster, making me jump nervously. I turned around quickly, laughing at my nervousness, and saw Jenny at the foot of the stairs. I smiled at her and she smiled back at me warmly.

"Did you sleep well?" I asked, inviting her to sit down in front of her piping hot chocolate.

"Like a baby, as strange as that is."

"I'm glad you were able to rest. Have some toast," I said, handing her a piece of warm toast.

She buttered it slowly and put it back down on the table. Her hands were holding her cup of hot chocolate and she seemed to be thinking. I looked at her, raising my eyes, and she continued:

"How long is it going to take?"

"What do you mean." I answered, though I already knew what she would say.

"How long before she'll come and get me?"

"Maybe... Maybe she won't come."

"She'll come. Maybe not tonight or tomorrow, but she'll come. She came for Kenny and Tom so she'll come for me too."

I tried to reassure her without really believing what I was saying. I told her that maybe she forgot about her seeing that she wasn't home anymore and maybe she didn't have to be afraid now. And this was probably right. After all, she slept well last night, didn't she? Had she wanted to kill her, after all the witch could have come to my house or to her house, witches can do those things. I didn't understand why she nodded her head. Did I succeed in reassuring her even just a little or was she just trying to put an end to this conversation.

Jenny went to the bathroom to get ready for school and I cleared the table. A half-hour later, we were both ready to leave. Before that though, my mom had filled our lunch bags with a delicious lunch and after-school snack for both of us, bringing me a non-negligible dose of comfort.

We walked to school, almost in silence. Even though neither of us mentioned it, we were both afraid there'd be a new tragedy when we got there. But we also both knew that Jenny was the next one on the list. I shivered despite myself, thinking back to that horrible nightmare. Or perhaps it was just because a cool breeze had sprung up? We got to the corner of the street where Amy lived and I was anxious to see her. Amy was my stability, my essential connection to reality. We turned into her street, with its beautiful tall oaks on each side. I walked faster and faster. I wanted to see her, I had to see her. My nightmare surfaced again, I rememorated her little face eaten by the worms. Apprehension invaded my spirit and I couldn't contain it. My stomach twisted and turned, trying to push it out, but to no avail. I started to run, I heard Jenny shout something out behind me, probably asking me why I was in such a hurry. I gasped when I saw the policemen in front of Amy's house. Her mom was screaming in the yard while two men were carrying out a little body covered with a white sheet on a stretcher towards the ambulance. I fell onto my knees on the sidewalk. We had succeeded in drawing the witch's attention away and saving ourselves, but all we did was divert her attention towards my best friend.

Sleep Tight

Written with Albert Spano.

"I think nighttime is dark so you can imagine your
fears
with less distraction."
Bill Watterson

– 1 –

I learned of my promotion two weeks ago and it will be effective in just a few hours. When I got the news, it was like a taste of eternal life. Like drinking from Christ's cup. I'd be strong and powerful, but above all, I'd have money. I'd wanted this job ever since I started working here. Things actually did go quickly though: in just a few months, I'd eliminated my rivals, discarded the dead wood, and cleared the hurdles obstructing my path to the top. Now, I've reached my goal. Ever since the promotion was announced, I've been terribly excited. I'm ready to rumble. The mail started with 'Dear All,' and ended with 'We wish him success in this endeavor, for him, for us, for our Company.'

An unlimited satisfaction. It woke me up again last night, undoubtedly the pride of my accomplishment. Sleeping through the night is now but a fleeting memory. It's true though that my brain is occupied by its new responsibilities. The assistant manager of an international company: the apotheosis of my entire career. No more open-spaces with the commoners. The new director that I would be would have director's privileges: a private office on the top floor overlooking the Seine River, a parking spot, with such a high salary and bonuses I wouldn't even know what to spend my money on.

Money. Lots of money. Money like I had never earned in my life, and which, little by little populated all my uncontrollable thoughts. I can't help but imagining the beautiful Mercedes coupé that I'd buy as soon as the first euros were transferred into my bank account, even though I don't care about cars and don't even like to drive. *"Your parking spot..."* That's what I remember, and what, amongst other things, was fueling my thoughts... I don't have a car yet, I haven't started my new job either and nonetheless I already feel richer and stronger.

Wide rims, metallic paint, leather seats, dashboard from exotic wood... A blatant status symbol. I didn't even want one actually. But my brain, and I couldn't control it - it was longing to possess it. To such a point, like I said before, that my nights had become the continuity of my days, a peculiar strength preventing me from being able to rest.

Sunday morning. 3. I'm trying to quell this cerebral activity that no longer wants to go into sleep mode. I open my eyes, looking at the ceiling in my room and I know they won't close again. I get up and sit down on the couch in the living room, hoping that this attempt at diversion will trick my rebellious spirit. I turn on the TV, naively believing in its sleep-inducing powers.

Sports broadcasts are being shown in a loop. Minutes, then hours go by, I now know all the results by heart, but sleep continues to elude me.

"It's a done deal now, the Paris Saint Germain soccer league will now longer train at the Camp des Loges; our capital's club will be leaving Saint-Germain-en-Laye after 32 years. See you then in Poissy for new adventures, a brand-new training center now awaits our soccer players who presented the press with their new jerseys. At home, the club will be wearing its traditional colors and when playing away from home, the club will wear a new white jersey."

And that's exactly when it happened. One word — *white* — pronounced for the twelfth time that night. And while I could still hear the broadcaster's voice bouncing off the walls, the curtain in the living room rose and suddenly I couldn't breathe.

The window wasn't open and there was no breeze in the living room, so why was this white drape dancing around in the air and stealing my oxygen? I tried to open my mouth to chug a puff of life-saving air, but to no avail. I have to breathe, even just a little...

I'm at the bottom of a river without water. An invisible current is dragging me under and preventing me from surfacing. The drape is flying around in the living room, just as if it is driven by its own force. I can't move. I can't even budge. I'm chained to my own body. The drape is flying towards me now. I try to take a deep breath, to scream, but no noise comes out of my mouth. My vocal chords are fading away in my throat. The sounds are dying in my head.

The drape is gone now but someone is watching me. I can feel him and I'm afraid.

Someone broke into my apartment. What does he want? How did he get in? When I got back from work, everything seemed normal. Was he already hidden somewhere? Scrutinizing me and waiting for the right moment to do his dirty deed? Impossible. The drapes aren't thick enough to hide someone behind them. And even if this someone could have succeeded in eluding me, he would have taken advantage of the first part of the night when I had dozed off to accomplish what he had set out to.

He's behind me! I can hear him breathing. His warm breath is blowing through my hair. He's stealing this air that I need so much.

I want to turn my head around so I can see him, but my neck is stuck, it's anchored into this armrest that is nothing more than a continuation of my body. I'm going to die here, asphyxiated. Frozen into this couch like a cold body in its shroud. No witnesses, a pathetic death.

He's stealing my oxygen and spitting it out again on my head. He likes playing with me, I can feel it. I know it.

I'm scared stiff. My muscles have turned into stone. As stiff and hard as concrete. A concrete block someone laid and forgot about.

I'm going to die here alone and never even get to drive my beautiful German sports car.

Breathe in through your nose!

I have to forget this guy behind me. Just for a few seconds so I can concentrate on my nostrils. I have to do this; my life depends on it.

I try to close my eyes, but my eyelids won't obey. The thirteenth sporting journal tonight is beginning, I can't help but reciting the results in my head.

Concentrate!

My nose! Where is my nose? Help!

I'm going to die and someone will find my body here on the couch. The putrid stench of my decomposed flesh will alert one of my neighbors, or perhaps my absence from the office will worry my colleagues before Mother Nature has the time to carry out its sordid work. *"And he didn't even have time to take advantage of this office overlooking the Seine River and the rooftops of Paris*," my successor will say, quietly thanking the gods of fate who allowed him to climb up to the summit.

My brain is freezing in my skull.

A death rattle can be heard in the room. A guttural and deep one.

A smoker unveiling his tobacco-filled glottis.

I'm horrified.

On the scale measuring fear, I'm balancing on the highest rung, the one that I never in my whole life would have dreamed of playing a tightrope walker on. With a fleeting moment of lucidity though, I try one last time to slowly concentrate on my nose. Trying to calm down in this horrific moment is my only hope of survival.

And air suddenly does penetrate into my nostrils. I feel like someone who nearly drowned and who finally rose to the surface of the water. Oxygen enters into my lungs so quickly that my chest is burning and my bronchial tubes are enflamed.

Like I took a breath for the very first time. Like I was born again.

The air flows into my lungs and it's marvelous. I might not die tonight after all.

"Of course not, you're not going to die tonight," a reassuring voice deep inside me says.

Even though I had recovered a part of my

respiratory capacities, fear was still eating away at my gut. I can hear him and he's right behind me.

Who is this intruder? What does he want from me?

A movement. Behind me. An imperceptible shift of the air I can feel on my head.

I think he's getting up.

Fear gives way once again to sheer terror. The sound of it is galloping through my thoughts.

My mouth is invaded by saliva and the metallic taste of fright has filled my swollen and sticky tongue. A cascade of silent screams pours through my head and my whole body is now immersed.

In the shadows, I can see his two eyes above my head. He's tilted his upside-down face towards mine and is staring at me.

This may seem strange to you, but I wanted to know what time it was now. Was dawn about to break? Would he then disappear like a vampire, as soon as the first beams of sunlight would come into the room? Would he go back into his world where fear is a second skin, a world where death is a way of living?

Why doesn't he say anything?

Is he a man like myself, a man who is now smiling at me in the shadows?

I thank the Lord for this air I am now breathing, even though the impression of suffocating has not yet completely disappeared.

A meagre reprieve.

Who are you?

His beady eyes kept starting right into mine and there was a hideous mocking grin distorting the bottom of his face.

He's not moving. Not talking. Not even touching me... He's savoring this.

His victory?

I'd like to spit in his face. But why are you standing still like that? And who are you? Who the hell are you? A jealous colleague, a burglar, a sick sex offender? What have you got against me?

A cowardly rage is stirring in my gut. There's no wrath in it, merely fear nourished by these eyes staring at me. By this smile that seems to defy me. By this breathing hammering on my skin.

I'm alone, frozen in my movements tonight.

And then suddenly, he starts to move. He wants to show me something.

Through the pale moon shining through the living room windows, I can imagine his hand, opening and closing, just like some sort of magician who's warming up his hands before going on stage.

His smile is stretched over his jaw.

The atmosphere is heavy, impure, and foul. What is now breathable will soon no longer be so. This I can feel.

His hand slowly comes towards me and squeezes my nostrils.

I can no longer breathe.

-2 —

Last night's events totally wiped me out, nonetheless my mind of a winner overcame this and my terrible fatigue did not prevent the total success of the extraordinary General Meeting held on this Monday to confirm my promotion. In front of all the employees, my management was a savant and perfect blend of motivation, goals, figures, bonuses and stress, all garnished with a hint of fear, distilled in all of those not welcoming me with open arms. Obviously, all the senior executives were also there. I wanted to embody success, a new breath of life in our company. A whole day talking, explaining, saying and repeating why the curve must increase, showing everyone my office door *that will always be open. And rest assured that your proposals will always be welcomed.*

During the meeting I couldn't help but thinking about what had happened last night. I left my office at about 8 pm and went straight to the police station. After waiting for a good half an hour during which I used my cell phone to answer my mails, I was able to speak to a police officer about what happened and then I went to get some sushi at Toyama's.

It's 11:40 pm according to my phone's blue-white screen. Its weak light is shining on my bedroom's ceiling that I'm staring at, waiting and hoping for sleep. This time I won't go to the living room couch.

I was still completely traumatized by the man who broke into my apartment on Saturday night. I didn't know who to talk to about this, so I decided to talk to someone I didn't even know. The idea of hopping into a cab and telling an unknown driver about this tempted me. But I was afraid that this story would be distorted with all the miles that the cab would continue to do once I had left.

I decided to let my fingers do the walking and went to the Yellow Pages. I wanted the best professional possible. I wanted the one whose fees guaranteed me value for money. The one whose bill would ensure his competence. *What a cliché.* I still got a good one though.

"No break-in: no offense."
But I had explained to the policeman how sure I was that someone had broken in to my place the other night. But he continued to shake his head, lips pursed and a slightly exasperated look, while repeating, *"No break-in, no offense."* I turned around and slowly walked to the exit of the police station, my head bowed in resignation and with a lump in my throat by anger when one of the policemen said, turning towards me: *"I'm sorry*

that we can't take your complaint, but I think you should try to see someone, you look like you need to talk to someone..."

Of course I need to talk to someone! About what happened during this strange night. About the unhealthy and insidious thing inside my body. A permanent malaise, a constant discomfort that spoiled the pleasure of my huge promotion.

On Monday evening, after the police station and sushi bar, I consulted forums, read the remarks and comments of dozens of patients, and finally one name stood out from the others: Doctor Samuel.

I got an appointment on Tuesday morning at 9:15.

And here I was, in bed, two days after this much-awaited appointment, lying down and worried, my eyes staring up at this white ceiling that looked like a sky where the blue had been swept away. *"Hang in there,"* the psychotherapist told me. *"You always end up falling asleep."*

I still didn't know what to make of this first session of psychoanalysis. Perhaps it was the first step in a new experience. I've never found it easy to talk about my life to someone I don't know, especially when the one you're talking to doesn't reciprocate. But I once had a similar situation. It was when I was a teen-ager, for my solemn Communion. The priest had called us one by one into the confessional, asking us each to confess to our sins before receiving the body of Christ for the first time. *"My son, I'm listening. Don't be afraid. Tell me what sins you are asking to be pardoned."* I didn't know what to say. I didn't have anything to be pardoned for. I was a good boy, I studied hard and loved my family. Why did he insist that I confess sins that I didn't have? *"Everyone has something to confess,"* we learned in catechism. But I never did anything wrong. Never. So rather than saying nothing and having the priest get mad at me, I lied. I invented a type of evil that didn't exist inside me, and I resented him for this. He turned a nice little lamb into a ram with cloven hooves. I was a good little boy, and this so-called 'man of God' shoved me into the wayside, because according to him and his God, we're all guilty before being tried.

The psychologist didn't ask me about any of this stuff, though I'm sure that had I confided my most shameful sins to him, he would have absolved me of all of them like a divine personage exercising his all-powerful omnipotence between the four walls of his cabinet. His cabinet, let me tell you about it. I had barely set foot on the thick Turkish carpet on the floor and had just gone through the door when I was hit by a strong odor. As if all the other scents had been sucked out of this room by this olfactive fog in the atmosphere. A strong odor of a winter scent with peppery and juicy notes. In spite of this though I felt happy to have the ability to smell this unsettling odor and thanked the doctor for his heavy hand on the perfume bottle, thus giving me the possibility of trembling at the very thought that the air, on one night at the beginning of the week, was lacking.

My room's ceiling represents a dome without sides. There are no walls and it seems to be suspended above me and my body lying on the sheets.

My throat is dry and I seem to feel the peaked tongue of anxiety licking my bowels. I can't help but think of this priest and what he made me do, of this psychologist who looked at me behind his horn-rimmed glasses and this ceiling that seems to be getting closer and closer to me.

Perhaps I should hide behind the living room couch?

"You always end up falling asleep," repeats Doctor Samuel's deep voice subconsciously.

I can't say if I actually fell asleep. I feel like I'm floating in a semi-conscious state, between dreams and reality.

The ceiling is watching me and enveloping my body like a lead case the covers a coffin that nothing must escape from, even after death. My eyes are scotched to it and can't look away.

I hear something humming. Like something started up someplace near me.

I'm not sleeping. No, I'm not sleeping, it's

impossible. I can hear this sound much too precisely in my ears to be sleeping. Cables grating against steel, the clicking of metallic pieces interlocking one into another, creaking of pullies screeching against my eardrums. An auditive torture. Some mechanism has started working. My cerebral capacities are at the maximum and my consciousness at its paroxysm. This can't be possible.

My eyes try to focus and trick the darkness of my room. And the unthinkable happens: that mechanism... the ceiling is lowering itself. There's no doubt about this. It's lowering itself noisily, screaming out its intentions through this horrible noise of steel being mishandled. It's screaming out its wish to pose itself on me. To lean on my body, pressing it against itself, though in theory anyway, it's an inanimate thing. The sentence is not subject to appeal: I'm doing to die, squashed in my own bed. A clean and dramatic end. An inexorable outcome. An unforgiving conclusion.

This infernal machine must be stopped! There must be a button somewhere to turn off this evil machine! Unless... Unless I get out of here. Right! If I can't stop the gears of this pernicious demon, perhaps I can try to escape. Suddenly rip off the linin sheets that cover my once-again martyred body and flee far from here.
I was going to try to get up when my muscles froze. I immediately recognized this peculiar odor pounding against my sinuses. An easily

recognizable fruit and peppery note. A mixture of mandarins and marketing.

You son of a bitch! You didn't come here to help me! Not at all! The arm in control of this machine the Devil made is yours! Son of a bitch! You didn't think I'd recognize you, did you? You were betrayed by your horrible perfume. You didn't actually think you'd be able to assassinate my anonymously?

Help! Can't anyone hear me?

It's like the sheets are glued to my body. But hadn't I shrugged them off before? Did I? I don't know anymore. I can't put my thoughts in order anymore or remember anything. But who cares? I think the air is going away again.

Please I'm begging you - not last night's nightmare once again!

My cries for mercy remained unheard and the powerful odor penetrated even deeper into my nostrils, expelling the oxygen I needed to remain alive. While the air was escaping from my body, the ceiling continued its inexorable descent towards me. The farther it came, the less I could breathe. The sheets refused to budge. I'm like a drowning person lost in a sea of cotton, trying to fight the waves and extricate myself from these whitecaps hitting against my mattress, now soaked in my own sweat. I'm going to die. Crushed by the weight of this concrete structure. Without even understanding how this could have happened. Doctor Samuel came in and he changed the ceiling's structural frames. MY ceiling, how could he have done this?

It will soon be over. Now my ceiling is just a few inches from my face. My nose, martyred since last Tuesday, will be the first to experience the ingenious atrocity that this psychologist dreamed up, one whose pathology measured up and even exceeded those of his worst patients. And then I thought of something: my future Mercedes sports car. Crushed into a cube by the teeth of a grinding machine. I'd wanted this damn car so much and I'm going to end up just like it... Life and death... Isn't it ironic? But I'm not a car! I don't want to end up like some crushed ice, scattered here and there, moist and dripping onto the rough sheet wrapped around my body.

I'm screaming inside myself. Only a weak sound comes out of my lips though.

A paltry cry for help.

I'm dying.

I'm suffocating and soon my lungs will be empty. The ceiling lowering itself onto me will finish the job. It'll make sure I never get up again.

This time it's over. But in one last attempt to refute this resignation, I try to turn my head one last time. Spare my nose from suffering even more than it has in the past few days. Save time. Even just a few seconds. I won't avoid dying but I'll steal a few fleeting moments of survival from my assassin. Plus, I'm afraid this is going to hurt. My nose is so thin and fragile that it'll break into a thousand pieces as soon as the concrete touches it. My cartilages will explode, one after another and each nerve will convey unbearable pain to my brain. If I can get my head to turn, my cheek will be the first to go. Suppler, more fat in it, less sensitive. Less suffering.

My head is turning! Salvation came from my left side and my jaw sank into the feathery pillow. But this gigantic effort used up the tiny bit of energy and oxygen I had left. Now nothing was obeying me, save my neck. My members are tetanized. Like fossilized in the mattress. I don't have any fuel left for anything else. But who cares? If I don't die smothered, I'll die crushed. My head flattened against my pillows on my bed, trying to gain a few more seconds of respite, like an interlude before death, the horror of this situation terrifies me: death is looking me straight into my eyes. I don't believe it. All of this is impossible.

The wooden confessional trap is swinging in front of me, back and forth through the weak blond beams from the moon that that has just risen. No air is present now in the room and it seems to be dancing around in a gravity-free atmosphere. Just for a second I forget about the white dome that will soon be pressing down on my cheek, full of hopes and joy that I'll be able to leave this hell on earth. I have to dive into it! But I can't move - it's impossible!

And just like a prayer that was somehow

heard, a hand comes out of the trap and grabs my body. A silent cry of terror pierces my spirit which now is at the edge of a bottomless pit. My entire life is merely the cold result of the sum of all my errors.

The sticky odor seems to be more pronounced now, if that was even possible.

My head is killing me. But that won't last for long. It'll soon look like a too ripe piece of fruit that someone threw onto a wall to burst it open.

Thousands of questions are going through my head, thousands of questions in a tenth of a second. A violent collision rattles my whole nervous system from my toes up to the very top of my skull. I feel like screaming, insulting, spitting, breathing — *Oh ! Jesus Christ just let me breathe - let me see my parents - my mother .... mom, I want to see you one more time... —*

It's time now! The beginning of the culminating moment, when the largest fireworks are shot off, the opening day of the play!

The ceiling is touching my cheek now and starting to press down on my cheekbone. Horrified, I note that it's cold and pitiless.

With the pressure, my skin is distorted, my bones are cracking.

I try to close my eyes, as if that could lessen the pain. But they remain open, as if I was forced to watch this show, sitting right in front of the stage. There's no way I could miss even a second of this exceptional performance, one that was being given in my honor. I can feel my eyes rolling about in their orbits, refusing to pop out. I want to cry, but I can't muster up any tears.

And then the hand that came through my childhood confessional appears and gives an order. It points a finger towards the ceiling which stops. A windfall! The ceiling is obeying this hand that came from who knows where! The hand that stopped its descent with just a finger. Is this a friendly hand? I feel relieved though the lack of air is still fanning the fire in my lungs. Time seems to be suspended. As if the hands on a clock were floating in the air.

With an abrupt and precise gesture, this saving hand comes towards me. It wants to catch me and pull me out of this trap! I'll finally be alright! I still feel like crying and shouting, but this time because of relief. And then, just like a slap on my cheek so I'd shut up, the index and thumb come closer to me and this hand, the hand I'd thought was a friendly one, slowly and almost tenderly, squeezes my nostrils shut.

Game over.

Far away, I can hear mocking laughter.

-3 —

Wednesday after work. The beginnings of a migraine are circling around in my head.

I'm now three days into my new job as the manager of the division that I've been working in for nearly five years. This promotion is what I've wanted all these years. Like I've won the finals after a long and unrelenting combat. A trophy that I'm holding up in my arms after jumping over all the hurdles, one after another, after having elbowed away all the other sharks swimming around me, ready to gobble me up without any remorse. I won, and I'm proud of what I've done.

Proud. Happy. But stressed.

My office is a huge room with an immense window. Six hundred and fifty square feet overlooking Paris. A desk made from precious wood in the middle of the room, a hand-knotted wool carpet on the spic and span hardwood floor and a comfortable armchair so I can remain seated for hours on end while I work with my Excel files. My armchair is covered with top quality black patinated leather that's smooth and comforting when you touch it. On the left side when you come in, there's a small couch facing the immense skyline. That's where I seat my best clients — *the others can sit in the armchairs facing me* — and in front of this sofa, a glass coffee table. A few good bottles are hidden underneath, priceless assets to help my negotiations go the way I want them to.

My arms folded in front of these huge transparent walls, I admire the view of the rooftops reddened by the setting sun. A feeling of omnipotence invades me. I dominate the world —

my world — arms folded, standing in my Italian suit and its impeccable cut, I'm relishing this moment.

I got home late tonight. But getting home late is just the very beginning of my new daily routine. As soon as I walked into my apartment, the pressure suddenly fell, to give way to an indescribable fatigue. I was much too tired to do anything at all, except take a quick shower and lay down on my bed, my body still warm and humid, simply wrapped up in my gray cotton dressing gown. I laid my head down onto two plump pillows I'd put one on top of the other. My body loosened up and evacuated all the tension accumulated throughout the day.

Those endless business lunches that I had to go to were now a part of my daily routine, just like the marketing or sales meetings. Hours spent in restaurants with other men in perfectly tailored suits. Individuals with lots of responsibilities who never had to be accountable for their acts. Bosses swimming in the troubled waters of their imperfections. I'd soon be just like them. Arms folded behind my picture window, I'm slowly starting to join this class of individuals, ones who believe that the world is their own oyster, just because they look down on it.

Important decisions, paltry initiatives.

I'm them, they're me.

I even *have* an assistant. *"What was your*

name again Miss?"

Am I going to become an asshole just because I work with assholes? I'm sure you already know that answer though.

Today I sidestepped this. One more big client in a four-star restaurant. A few juicy contracts to discuss and negotiate. I didn't go though. I sent my assistant, Deriviere. He's a good guy, Deriviere, I trust him. But mostly I didn't have a choice. I had to see this doctor immediately.

I wasn't convinced by my psychotherapist and wanted a second opinion. I was able to get an appointment with Dr. Dray, a general practitioner who had worked in this neighborhood for ages.

After having listened to me, I asked me to lie down on the consultation table. He took my blood pressure, listened to my heartbeat, monitored my breathing.

- "Do you smoke? Do you do any sports? Do you eat balanced meals?"
- « No. »
- « Are you stressed? Do you work too much? And do you eat fatty food? »
- « Yes. »

He came around the table and stood in front of me.

- "I think that you're suffering from sleep apnea. It's a respiratory distress syndrome and the respiratory flow momentarily stops. And in the long run, if it's not treated, this is something that can be dangerous.

He went behind me and put his cold stethoscope on my back.

- "Breath with your mouth... Inhale... Exhale... And now with your nose. Inhale... Exhale everything..."

Your nose. When I heard him say that, my whole body was covered with goosebumps.

I actually trembled.

- "Did you have an accident? Did you fall? Can you remember any shock you had on your face?"

I shook my head from left to right.

- "From what you're saying," Dr. Grey continued," I'd bet that it's a deviated nasal septum. You'll have to do some complementary exams and consult a specialist in sleep apnea. And if this is the problem, it's quite normal that you haven't been sleeping well. Lie down on the table," he ordered.

My eyes are looking at the ceiling. It's white. Like at my place, like all the ceilings.

The doctor is sitting on his stool, behind me. I can't see him. All I can see is the white reflection of a horizontal structure that's coming closer to me. I beg a God that I don't believe in to save me from the terror I went through the other night. But he remains deaf to my cries for mercy and the ceiling comes down again, much faster this time. The room is silent, as if an invisible force has swallowed everything, even the sound of silence.

An evil soul reigns here.

I panic. I shout.

The ceiling is going to fall into my open mouth. It's there, so close that it's fuzzy in my eyesight. It's distorting so that it will penetrate me and take possession of my body. This concrete enemy is trying to invade me and is going to succeed. This time I won't survive. There's no way out.

I don't understand what's going on here.

My neck hurts.

Where's my doctor?

The pain is now unbearable. My neck is rigid.

My senses have disintegrated, I've become a shred, a left-over, an end-of-life product.

My head hits down on the surface of the table, someone must have grabbed the pillow it was lying on. Acute and muted pain shoots through my head. I'd like to mass my temple with my hand, but my arms are imprisoned.

The ceiling is already in my throat. Its concrete has a horrible taste. A mixture of gravel and sand covers my tongue, I feel like vomiting. Vomiting the matter, vomiting the stones, vomiting my guts out to free myself from this unbearable feeling. For one brief second, I've got the hope of believing that by holding my breath, I'll avoid breathing in all this toxic matter into my body, but of course, that's just a pipe dream. The farther the ceiling melts into me, the more my body solidifies, as if its particles were fixing themselves in my entrails. I'm muting, no longer a man made from bones and water, turning into a guinea pig victim of a dangerous doctor with a twisted mind.

I'm no longer sure that I'm living, but I'm not sure either that I'm already dead. I'm travelling between two worlds, in transit in a frightening place where there's no one else to keep me company. I'm waiting, terrified, to board for this unknown destination that fills me with fear. It'll be a one-way ticket. No one buys a round trip here. I'm dying.

And then like the other night, the flow of concrete halts its funeral march inside me. This deafening silence that was bursting my eardrums suddenly snapped. My own voice is bouncing of the stifling surface around me, just like a needle going through a child's ball. Air is coming! Jesus Christ, huge breaths of cool air are coming into my lungs just like waves beating onto the sand. My whole throat is once again welcoming the air finally coming in. I'm sincerely overjoyed and my throat has been cleaned of this atrocity. There had been dust down there, the acrid taste of clay, the feeling of having a thick coat of concrete on my tongue: all of this disappeared in a snap of a hand. Life-saving air came into me and my body changed into a fireworks show. I'm a celebration in my own right. My members are still immobile, glued to the sides of my body, but I can't expect everything at once: God is not a magician.

When I write these lines, it's a sure thing that death hasn't caught up with me yet. But what will happen at the end of this story?

I feel a caress on my skin. Hands? Yes, hands, and a woman's hands at that. They're coming and going on my neck and I have no problem feeling them even though I can't see them. They're soft and they smell good. I'm imagining them with a perfect manicure: a divine sensation in this horrible nightmare.

They're going from my chin to the base of my neck. A crazy feeling. My trachea, which just a few seconds ago was clogged by a flood of chemical matter, is now once again a haven of peace. Air is circulating perfectly and freely. I'm not used to it and I'm enjoying this feeling; it's almost like a discovery. No one ever massages your larynx, they always content themselves with your back, legs or neck, but never your larynx... this is a unique feeling. The hand continues to massage my skin, but now I think that it's the thumb doing all the work in this incredible massage. I know, because the area where there's pressure is wider, and the hand is closed. Just a thumb rubbing me, Jesus Christ, does this feel good!

The finger continues its heavenly affair and I just go with the flow. Its rubbing circles around my Adam's apple now. No one has ever done that for me before. I feel like I'm experiencing new pleasures. Something totally new. It's both exciting and frightening. Because at each rub, the pressure is a little stronger. No one has ever caressed me like that... but then again, no one has ever tried to kill me.

The hand has stopped giving me its pleasures and now only the thumb is rubbing on my Adam's apple. I don't understand. There's pain: simple, increasing and cruel. Pain accompanied by asphyxiation. Why did they clean me up then? Just to give me a little respite? Who is having fun with this little sadistic game?

I'm still immobile here on the doctor's table, strapped to this torture bed that a doctor with feminine fingers has. The ceiling has disappeared, but a foreign object is pressing down through my skin and I'm experiencing unbearable pain. Someone's attacking me, compressing me, strangling me. My mouth opens and at the same time someone is pressing down on my throat. And the more my mouth opens, the less air comes in. Ironic, isn't it? I'm drowning without a drop of water in my lungs.

It's still impossible for me to move, but I have to know who hates me so much that they're killing me. I try to look behind me, and though my skeleton is still bedded into a type of void, I order my eyes to fight one last battle. I try to control their revulsion. I send them to my back, asking them to look behind me to see who's hiding there, who wants to hurt me so much. I don't want to die without knowing the truth!

He (or she) thinks that I've passed out, because my aggressor's pression lets up. My eyes rolling around probably made him think that the end is now near. But nothing is really ever over. My eyes continue their route and persist in meeting the challenge I've given them. My head is aching, now joined by an ophthalmic pain. Knives are poked into my eyes, but their blades aren't enough to make me blind.

I can finally see you!

Her ! I'm devastated, ravaged...

Why?

What's your name again Miss?

-4 —

10:20. Thursday morning. I'm running late.

The front of the subway car is crowded. Right at the front to exit quickly, I'll just have a few feet to go before walking up the stairs and seeing sunlight. I feel a bit peculiar. I'm going to consult at specialist, following my doctor's orders - *"We need some complementary exams. I'll send you to one of my colleagues at Pasteur Hospital."*

I feel like I'm waging a war. The psychologist, the GP, the specialist... all this is wearing me down. I don't feel like going to this Super Doctor whose exceptional talents were lauded by his less-gifted colleague, who would probably be spending his whole life in his little dusty office.

I refuse this. Not because I feel it's absurd, but because the only idea I can concentrate on right now is my meeting with my Super Client: Mr. Smith. There's no room in my brain for anything else. Mr. Smith, from Smith Inc. He's got an idea I can't stop thinking about: an idea of a merger and acquisition of his English insurance company, and he contacted me to take care of this. So the doctors, the specialists and even the specialized specialists....

It's true that the past few days have not been easy. I explained all that to the psychologist. Someone, a man or a lady, I don't know, came to my house and gassed me. Nothing was stolen in my apartment, so the cops just sent me back home. But I have chest pain. My thorax tightens and the pain I have in my throat is still acute.

"Except for perhaps sleep apnea, I can't see anything wrong. "You're in good health," my general practitioner confirmed. Or maybe my psychologist. Or was it one of the cops? I don't know anymore. But it's no big deal. I have to concentrate on my meeting with Smith and not losing even a drop le my energy by thinking of this infimal detail.

My thoughts however come back to that German sedan. I can. Because it's linked to the signature that Smith is going to put on our contract.

I asked my assistant, whose name I can never remember, to draw up a schedule for me. I needed to know exactly what order things were coming in and my schedule would be my reference in my action plan I'd set up for myself. A meticulous and detailed one. Not like this subway map I still can't understand. Had my action plan been as confused and approximate, I would have died a long time ago. I think it's the very first time I've paid such attention to all these multicolored lines on this sheet of paper. With locations of each station, their numbers, their entrances and exits, their connections and transfers and their train lines, black, thick and ugly. Just like multicolored streamers and confetti that you throw on December 31st or when someone is getting married. Just like a kid, I count the number of subway stations until I can get out of this underground hell. I say them out loud, playing a childish game that I have to say them all without taking a breath: *Convention, Vaugirard, Volontaire, Pasteur...*

The subway driver announces over the loud speaker: *"you're just a person on the tracks!*

I look around me. I feel like I'm sitting in the middle of my thoughts. And each thought has a different color, like each of these subway lines. Have you ever sat in the middle of your brain? A pleasant feeling. All these colors and all these lines. Once again, like all these multicolored streamers that take me from my turnover to my profit margin. Out loud I recite the indecent bonuses that'll be mine, I play a game of proudly spelling out these enormous amounts I'll soon have without taking a single breath.

You're just a person on the tracks!

Why is that subway driver talking to me? Did I do something wrong?

No, there's nothing really wrong my dear man, but your nocturnal experiences can be traumatizing, why don't you go see a psychologist?"

Jesus! I've already been to this damn psychologist! And not just him! A general practitioner too! And I'm going to consult a super specialist!

I'm talking out loud but no one seems to hear. They're all busy with their phones or their papers. Even people who aren't doing anything special are looking into nothing, as if they were rocked to sleep by the subway line and couldn't hear my protests.

Sir?

Who's talking to me?

Sir? Be careful!

What should I be careful of? We're at Pasteur. I hope I won't be wasting my time and this super doc will be able to tell me what's wrong...

Sir, be careful!

Did anyone ever cut one of your members off? It's pretty weird.

It was a clean cut though. Almost like a surgeon had done it.

It all happened so fast. I rushed out of the subway car and to make up for lost time, I had the ludicrous idea of crossing the tracks. Now I find it ludicrous, now that my arm has been cut off. But then I thought it was a good idea, and I wasn't risking anything. Not even for an instant could I have believed that such an unfortunate experience could happen to a guy like myself. I've got a high-responsibility job, a huge office, a 25-year old Scotch in my minibar and I were tailored Italian suits; life doesn't play tricks like this on someone as important as I am. But I guess that day it had decided that I'd be the exception.

I jumped off the platform once the subway had started up again, then I stepped over the first two tracks with no problem. But the third track seemed to have thought that things had gone too easily for my and deviously caught the tip of my shoe. I tripped and fell. Just like it had hoped. I was going to fall onto the track and electrocute myself but at the very last second I succeeded in twisting my body, so that I'd avoid it when falling. If I ever get a copy of the video surveillance film, I'll show it to you. You'll see how impressive this contortion was. Unfortunately, though I had succeeded in avoiding the electrical shock, I couldn't avoid landing on the subway track in front of me. My right arm on this mocking track didn't last an instant. It was suddenly cut off my body, escaping it to live its own life, far from my shoulder and my body which had always welcomed it without complaining.

I didn't even see any blood. A clean cut. Like when you're slicing ham. The pain, however, was atrocious. An unfitted pain, just like someone who was trying to shove a big squared into a small circle. And what's ironic about all of this is that it happened because I was going to see the specialist that my general practitioner recommended. Maybe I should change my doctor's appointment and get one with a prothesis specialist. When I was a kid, I watched *The Six Million Dollar Man*. If prices have decreased and Steve Austin isn't worth as much right now, with all the money that my bonuses will be bringing me, I'll be able to rival him. And I'll make sure my car is an automatic one, I've heard they're pretty good now. I've still got my common sense, I feel reassured.

I hear panicked voices.

Help... Pasteur... Horrible... Man on the tracks... fucking asshole, I'm going to be late...
Sir, Sir !

I'm sincerely sorry for what's happened. Everyone's going to be late now and traffic will be at a standstill for a long time. I hope they'll find my arm soon...

Sir !

I jump and open my eyes wide. I can make

out a silhouette wearing a cap. I totter, I reel. My arm is throbbing and I can hardly feel it. I had fallen asleep on it and cut off my blood flow. Standing up, hanging on to the metallic bar, my mouth is dry.

The silhouette is still talking to me. I'm trying to understand what it's saying. I close my eyes to think hard and try to emerge quickly. My eyesight quickly adapts to my environment. I swallow and I understand even before the man in front of me says anything. *Sir ! This is the end of the line. The subway is closing for the night, you can't stay here!*

I look at my watch and what I see seems impossible to me: it's 1:30 am and I've slept for fifteen hours, standing up in the last car, to the incessant round trips of Line 12, while a specialist was waiting for me for a sleep apnea test. Missed that appointment.

-5 —

When I moved into my new office, the first thing I did was to blow the 50,000 euros allocated to me by the Board of Directors so that I could organize and decorate my workspace as I wanted to. New furniture, a new carpet, exotic plants, an aquarium full of rare tropical fish, a minibar... Like the billionaire John Hammond in Jurassic Park probably said, "I spent without counting," and believe me, it's even better when the money you're spending isn't yours.

Moving in, rearranging.

I bought a beautiful four-place sofa that I had placed in front of the window. That place in my office was far from being innocuous. I use it as an ultimate weapon when negotiations aren't going well. *"Mr. Smith, why don't we take a short break on the couch here, and have a sip of this delicious 25-year-old bourbon?* Comfortably sitting down across from the view he had pretended not to see when he arrived, he would be interpreting his pocket symphony with one hand while the other was holding the glass full of this delicate beverage. Legs slightly spread and perfectly inserted into trousers by Armani, sitting straight up, eyes right on the Eiffel Tower, he was the other master of the universe. My *ego* from another country.

He'd let himself slide... carried by the city's waves. Forgetting for a few minutes that I was trying to stuff his head into this horribly expensive carpet. An efficient way to relax and to bring Mr. Smith into my camp to convince him. A subtle way of signing this contract with its conditions and terms that favored the company employing me. I wouldn't make a single concession. This agreement would be my agreement.

And if the discussions were really difficult? Then his fabulous black couch with its pure lines would come into play. He was my teammate, my hatchet man, my convertible Deriviere, my proposal that was impossible to say no to. But why my client ignored, was that should there be a true bone of contention, my company was ready for anything. Ready to give him much more than this breathtaking view giving him the impression that the most beautiful city in the world was up for grabs. My company would stop at nothing. No sacrifice was too high to satisfy the inexorable increase in profits. It was nourished by zeros stuck behind a figure and was never too full to continue. *"Mr. Smith, tonight you'll be with the most beautiful whore in Paris! A once-in-a-lifetime experience! And believe me my dear friend, you'll enjoy it. You'll be just like someone who struck a homerun with the bases loaded, his supporters cheering him on, and you want to know something? You're sitting on your playing field. Run a hand over this superb leather just as if you were running on the grounds of the baseball field. Run your fingertips over the Italian lining, which has been sewn just like your expensive suits. Let your head rest just like you're driving your sportscar, when your head is heavy and your nape is tight. Now imagine the new man that you'll soon be as soon as your put your signature on these couple of pages in the contract, the one that my assistant has prepared just for you. And in the meanwhile, Mr. Smith, let me step out for a minute, I need a break for this difficult discussion... You're*

I usually doze off a little in the afternoon. A power nap, just a few minutes, to recover. I undo the knot in my tie, take off my shoes, loosen my belt and lay my head down on the wide armrest in this sofa, my partner-in-crime for my greatest successes. I love winding down, nodding off. Trying to kill this damned fatigue that has been dogging me all day.

– WAKE UP!
I'm exhausted. This Smith guy is like a crocodile - you can only see his eyes above the surface of the water. I feel like I'm drowning in some strange-tasting liquid. My eyes are shut, but my eyelids horribly burnt off by it no longer prevent me from seeing. This pain is familiar.
And I'm drowning...

I've been here before. I recognize the leather couch. I'm at my office.
I keep sinking down into its depths and I don't understand. Straight down. I'm a pretty good swimmer but I sink without being able to surface again.
I can see Mr. Smith's body. He's floating around peacefully, his saw-blade grin staring at me through his mask. I'm immobile and he's winning this battle.
Once again my body is the tomb in which

I'm now so often trapped. I'm breathing in water now and can't do anything. *"Mr. Smith, you're a formidable adversary; I believe I've underestimated you."* I recognize this strange taste on my tongue, it's my bourbon. Is my descent into hell going to last 25 years too? There are bubbles between my lips; they're as yellow as stalks of corn. They slowly rise to the surface of the water, bursting into perfectly shaped cylinders that this Smith crocodile quickly gobbles up.

> *— I'm swallowing all of you right down my Dear Man!* he said sarcastically.

All I wanted though was to relax, just a few seconds. That's it. Was I asking too much? A simple round trip to dreamland to recover from a harassing battle fought with an important client. Why don't I have the right to breath, even for a few fleeting moments?

Something grabs me by the shoulders.

— WAKE UP!

This is impossible. I'm dying and you can't come back from death.

Liquid into liquid. A nice fish with multiple warm colors swims past me. He looks at me with his keen eyes that I compare to eggs, they seem so huge. I suddenly realize that I'm still sinking and that I'm drowning amid the exotic fish in this aquarium in the middle of my office.

Then I lose track of time, of balance and space and a black shroud covers the light that was coming through the water molecules. It's now dark and I can't see anything. No office, no fish, no aquarium. Just a void and I. I think I'm experiencing what is called a 'blast effect,' this suspended moment in time right after a bomb explodes. A tunnel between reality and the other reality that you go through and get lost in. Total amnesia of your senses that lasts a few seconds. I'm not just simply drowning in my aquarium or in my up-market bourbon, I'm in the blast effect and can't distinguish what's true or what's false. I don't even know if it's me who's breathing or if anyone at all is breathing here.

And then for the third time:

– WAKE UP!

Someone is beating me on the shoulders and shouting at me. And then I hear another voice. A lower and more soothing one suggesting that I think of my little toe. Of course! How could I have forgotten? I have to concentrate on my little toe if I want to regain control of my body. My instincts haven't abandoned me and I'm not giving up yet either. *"Smith, old chap, it's not over yet!"* I don't have much left - voices and one minute muscle - but I haven't said my last word.

With a great effort, I succeed in moving this infinitesimal part of my body. I focus all my attention on this miniscule part of myself which is the most important part of my body right now.

This ridiculous little pinkie is moving! Fuck it's moving! I've succeeded in winning, I try to control the sudden waves of rage within myself.

I can feel my foot and now my leg starts shaking. *"Mr. Smith, you can pack up your weapons now, it looks like the tide has turned!"* And life comes back with light. Light is flooding through my eyelids and I can once again see the world surrounding me. But at the very moment my joy exploded, the horror of the vision in front of my brutally shifted my emotions into chaos: *she's* standing in front of me and staring at me with her mean black eyes. I'm ridiculously small compared to *her*. Her enormous mouth is screaming out unbearably:

    – WAKE UP! she's shouting.

That Smith bastard!

She's shaking me up and down just as if I were a ragdoll. My neck is dislocated on the armrest of my couch. She pinches my nostrils and my mouth opens by reflex. It fills up with bourbon and this feels atrocious. Whole bottles are being poured down my throat, lighting it up just like a wildfire on arid land. This is torture and I'm ready to admit anything at all so it will stop. I can see my own body next to me. It's spitting out yellow and green streamers, vomiting colored ivy from some unknown place. Who cares though? The fact is that I'm puking up exotic plants in front of this bitch who's loving the way I'm suffering. She's killing me and she loves it.

Now I understand something. *She's* the one shaking me by the shoulders but someone else is shouting:

     –   WAKE UP!

And then there's a man's voice too: with slow, distinct and clear diction:

     –   You might wake up and then fall right back asleep. What's dangerous is that you begin confusing dreams with reality, darkness with light.

Who's talking to me?

     –   WAKE UP!

I want this lady to quit screaming at me and just shut up. I'm the master of my little toe, the master of darkness and light and you, you witch, I'm going to make you shut up for good. I ignore if it's because of my pinkie or if my leg is its joyful partner-in-crime, but I give her a good kick right in the middle of her fat face. There's no kidding around with my Weston's heel. The blow is direct, brutal and uncompromising. It hits my torturer's nose right in the middle and her cry of pain echoes through the room.

     –   SIR !

I recognize this voice!

Right when I was kicking her, that whore raised her hands to her face and because of the strength of the shock, her body teetered and in a useless attempt to recover her precarious balance, she hit the window with all her weight. Thousands of shrouds of glass shattered throughout the room and for a fraction of a second, they glittered like diamonds on her silhouette suspended in the airs. The Eiffel Tower, in the background, seems to dance in the middle of these ephemeral and cutting jewels. And then an atrocious cry. Net and distinct at first, then muffled and distant: *"What's your name again?'*

Am I a dog or a wolf? I don't even know myself.

Once again I can't fall asleep or I can't wake up. I don't know what I'm dreaming or what I'm living. The only thing I'm sure of happened several feet below my window. A sharp noise and sirens... the firemen, maybe the police, I don't know... people shouting for help.

My assistant is dead and I killed her.

– EPILOGUE –

Report written by Doctor Samuel, Psychiatrist.

Paris,
May 25, 2018

I didn't actually diagnose an illness, strictly speaking, for him. However, what I did diagnose that he was suffering from was a sleep disorder that we call 'sleep paralysis.' This is quite a common phenomenon, but my patient had abnormally high levels of this as he was a victim of it almost every time he'd fall asleep.

Sleep paralysis is a sleep disorder, or more precisely, parasomnia, which is characterized by the fact that the subject, when falling asleep, (hypnagogic paralysis) or waking up (hypnopompic paralysis), is incapable of moving any parts of his body, though he is totally conscious. If he maintains his composure, he can regain control of his body by concentrating on his little toe. Auditive or visual hallucinations as well as impressions of oppression, suffocation, presence of evil spirit and imminent death are often associated with this sensation of being unable to move. The subject, who cannot articulate any sounds and thus warn his friends or family, often feels a crippling sense of anxiety and fright linked to the panic this causes. This sleep disorder is due intrusions in REM or rapid eye movement sleep and the absence of muscular tonus which accompanies it during transitions between awakening and sleeping.

I had advised him to consult a specialist in sleep disorders, but I don't know if he did this. As time went by, he could no longer recover from these crises. It didn't do him any good to take naps during the day, as these disorders also occurred then. With such a huge deficit in sleep, he started thinking his dreams were real. He even told me once that *I* had attacked him! People you've seen during the day reappear as monsters at night. Everything was mixed up in his brain.

According to my hypothesis, the extreme state this patient was in was linked to the very stressful situation he had been experiencing for a while. As he had been recently promoted in his company to a top managerial position, the tension he had accumulated acted like a short circuit, disrupting the hormonal mechanisms required to correctly fall asleep and wake up. If I'm correct about the causes of his problems, the only solution would have been for him to step back from his functions for a while. It's often difficult to make these patients understand this, as the stress they're undergoing is often confused with the excitement that this new "professional challenge" has for them.

So, to conclude, I would just add that this

unfortunate gesture towards his assistant was merely a gesture of self-defense. She was trying to wake him up while he was in the midst of a crisis and he felt he was being attacked. What I mean there is he *actually believed* she was about to kill him.

There's no other explanation.

*